PACIFIC SHORES
- BOOK 3 -
Song of the Surf

Song of the Surf

Brynn STEWART

PACIFIC SHORES SERIES
Contemporary Christian Romance

Beyond the Waves – BOOK ONE

Caught in the Current – BOOK TWO

Song of the Surf – BOOK THREE

Written in the Sand – BOOK FOUR

Other books by Brynn Stewart

THE RIVERSONG SERIES
Contemporary Christian Romance

Angel Kisses and Riversong – BOOK ONE

Soft Kisses and Birdsong – BOOK TWO

Butterfly Kisses and Windsong – BOOK THREE

HEARTS OF HOLLYWOOD
Contemporary Christian Romance Novellas

My Blue Havyn – BOOK ONE

Mistletoe and Mochas – BOOK TWO

Kittens and Snow Flurries – BOOK THREE

MISTY COVE
Contemporary Christian Romance Novellas

The Heart of Christmas – BOOK ONE

The Wonder of Christmas – BOOK TWO

Galatians 6:9-10

Let us not become weary in doing good, for at the proper time we will reap a harvest if we do not give up. Therefore, as we have opportunity, let us do good to all people, especially to those who belong to the family of believers.

Chapter 1

Dakota Trask wanted to weep with exhaustion and Monday hadn't even closed up shop yet. The gloomy evening light reflected softly from her computer screen, doing nothing to disguise the evidence before her. She couldn't believe LoriMay had done this. Scooting her chair closer to her desk, she leaned toward the screen and clicked the button to tally the column of numbers again. She grunted when the sum came out the same as before. This couldn't be right, could it? The income showed a great deal more than the expense side, yet there were only a few cents left in the account according to the bank statement. So what had been purchased that hadn't been recorded? Her stomach rolled over on a wave of dread. Or at the very least, where had that withdrawal gone?

Dakota rubbed her temples. How was she to balance the ministry's budget when nothing seemed to be matching up?

She dropped her forehead onto her arm. "Lord, I

didn't sign up for this. Everything needs to be revamped and reassessed from the ground up!" If she had her car she would go see Pastor Mark right now. But she had loaned her car to Marie—whose Corolla had died again, and with her wedding less than a week away. So Dakota was stranded, for now.

But wait...she smacked her forehead and reached for her phone. The account was cloud-based, so she'd just call him and see if he had time to take a look. She pressed on Pastor Mark's name and listened as it rang. The phone rolled over to voicemail. Disappointed, she hung up without leaving a message.

Maybe it would be better this way. She'd finish her assessment and have a better understanding of exactly what expenses the church would be facing to keep House of Hope operational, and hopefully a report on where the missing money might have gone.

Outside the wind picked up and whistled through the eaves. Which reminded her of another thing she'd noticed. The roofing on the place was badly in need of replacement. And the faucet in the first bathroom down the hall dripped constantly, while the toilet in the other one did the same. She needed to put an announcement in the bulletin at church for some volunteer handymen to come out and do the repairs for her.

Where had LoriMay appropriated the money for such things? Dakota breathed out a sigh and forced herself to sit up. Whatever category it came out of was probably severely lacking in funds, if all the others could be a measurement.

A headache pinched at the front of her skull. "I need coffee." She pushed herself up from the desk and strode to the Keurig she'd bought with her own money. One sip of the brew from House of Hope's ancient yellowed Mr. Coffee machine that had added its own unique taste to every pot, and she'd made a special trip into town to buy a Keurig. She thrust her mug under the spout and popped in a K Cup, then pressed "brew."

The pot whirred and gurgled and began to drip.

She glanced at her watch. Another hour and Reece and Marie would be by to get her. Striding to the window, Dakota planted her palms against the sill and leaned close to look out at the rain-sodden evening. Dark clouds hung ominously, and lightning forked in a jagged shard across the distance. The percussion of thunder followed bare moments later. The trees along the back of the property cowered in the face of the Oregon coast wind, bending farther than she'd ever seen them go before. She leaned low and craned her neck to see the tops of the tall evergreens. One of them was swaying like a skyscraper in an earthquake.

"Wow. Crazy."

Mr. Novak's garbage can fell on its side and tumbled across his backyard, spilling garbage everywhere. It crashed to a stop against the split rail fence that separated his property from House of Hope's. Dakota sighed. Looked like tomorrow would be a day of cleanup.

A branch from one of the trees snapped and hurtled through the air straight toward her. Dakota ducked on reflex, but the branch lifted on a last-second current of air and skittered across the roof.

Dakota wrapped her arms around herself, thankful to be inside on such a terrible night.

Behind her the Keurig gave its last gurgling hiss, and the scent of fresh hot medium roast filled her nostrils, making her mouth water, and her tension ease at just the first whiff. A splash of peppermint mocha creamer and life would be righted again, if only for a few minutes. She opened the door of the mini fridge in the far corner and squatted down to snag the tall bottle of creamer from the back.

A huge crash shuddered through the building, and glass shattered. Adrenaline cinched up every muscle in her body. A wall of air slapped into her. Her hand slipped, and her forehead cracked into the corner of the fridge. She gave herself a little shake in an attempt to dispel the throbbing.

She'd somehow ended up on the floor. Had she really felt air? Another gust blew over her. Yes. Definitely. The chill sweep of icy Pacific wind, and the sting of slashing rain.

Rain?

She turned over slowly, groaning as pain sliced across her temple.

Where the corner of her office had been only moments ago, thick gray clouds hung low. Flying debris rocketed by, and a flash of lightning lit up the silver needles of water falling from the sky.

Her eyes widened.

What in the world...?

Pushing her hands into the carpet, she stood and lifted her gaze to assess what had happened. She staggered a sideways step. And blinked to clear her vision. Surely she was just seeing things. Disbelievingly, her focus swung back to the window she'd stood at only seconds before. The glass was now a web of fissures and jagged shards with a frame of mangled metal. But through a larger intact section, she could see that one of the trees that should be standing tall in the backyard was no longer there. She pressed a hand to the ache in her head. "Oh, wow. This is so not good!"

Her focus swung back to the missing corner of the house and began to pick out more details. Evening had fallen quickly, but the growing dusk did nothing to hide the serrated wall and splintered siding, the section of roof, and the large trunk of a tree with jagged branches that angled across her desk.

If I'd still been sitting there... She swallowed.

Rainwater began to puddle and seep across the carpeted floor.

She jolted herself to action. "I have to do something!" She scooped her hand back through her hair. What? "Think!"

A tarp. She knew there was a tarp on the shelf in the garage. It wouldn't stop all the water damage, but surely it would minimize it some.

My computer!

Only one corner of her monitor could even be seen. The rest of it lay smashed under a splintered beam, and she could see sparks pinging off of something. The desk lamp?

Electricity first. Then the tarp.

She tried to run down the hall toward the breaker box, but her legs trembled to the point of near uselessness, and it didn't help that she was wearing her favorite mint suede heels. She finally reached the gray metal panel at the end of the hall and flung it open, feeling pain zing across a couple fingers. Where was the main switch? Daddy had always said in an emergency to throw the main breaker. This box didn't seem to have one. Of course it didn't. This house was as ancient as the tree that had just tried to kill it. She gritted her teeth and quickly began switching everything off.

It wasn't till she got to the fuse that turned off the hallway lights that she realized she had no flashlight. She flipped it on once more and dashed back down the hallway to her office. When she jogged inside, her feet splashed against soggy carpet.

Hurry!

She yanked open the drawer next to the coffee maker and snatched out the flashlight, then ran back to the fuse box. She finished throwing all the switches and then darted down the hall, following the beam of her flashlight toward the garage and the tarp and ladder that were kept there.

She would have to open the garage door manually. Maybe she should run out to assess the damage first so she would know what tools and items to bring with her to fix the hole. She yanked on the cord to disengage the carriage from the garage door motor and then heaved up on the heavy wooden monstrosity. It groaned and rattled as it trundled upward, and before it was even halfway open, rain slanted into the garage.

She hesitated. Might as well keep as much of the water outside as possible. Leaving the door where it was, she ducked under it.

A man loomed in front of her – a dark bulky shape against the gray of the sky.

Her heart lurched into her throat, pinching off her screech as she swung hard with the flashlight.

But the man was quick and dodged inside her intended blow. He gripped her shoulders and gave her a slight shake. "Dakota, it's okay. It's just me. Justus Teague. Reece's friend. We met several months ago. Do you remember?" He pulled her back under the overhang of the eaves.

Dakota swallowed and wished she wasn't trembling so visibly. Did she remember? How could she forget meeting a man she'd called "calendar worthy" when she thought he wasn't around, only to have him overhear it and tease her about it?

Despite the chill of the wind and the pelts of rain that managed to find them in their meager shelter, she felt warmed by his presence. "Ju-Justus." It didn't matter that she'd been plotting all week how she would avoid him once he arrived in town for the wedding. She was just glad to see *someone.* "Can you help me? I need to—I'm not even sure what's happened—I was just running out to look. There was a crash, and rain, and sparks, and—" Words failed her, but her mind seemed to be working overtime. What was he doing here? Even if Reece and Marie had sent him, they hadn't planned to stop by for another hour.

Lightning flashed and Justus took her chin firmly in one hand and canted her head to an angle.

Dakota held her breath, chastising herself for noticing the wonderful spice-and-leather scent of his aftershave at this most inappropriate of moments.

With a concerned gaze fixed on her forehead, he slid his hand down her arm and pried the flashlight from her fingers. He lifted it and shone it just above her left eye. One of his brows quirked.

She angled her gaze upward to see what had drawn his attention. The beam of the flashlight illuminated a stream of red dripping from one of her eyebrows. She must have a little cut from where she'd hit her head on the fridge.

But she could deal with that later. They were wasting time here. She pushed his hands away from her face. "There's a hole in the ceiling. We need to get a tarp over it. But I need to go see the damage first." She made to dash past him even as sirens sounded just around the corner on Sand Dollar Lane.

He clasped her arm firmly and held her in place. "You aren't going anywhere. Let the fire crew take care of that for you. They'll have all the equipment to do what needs to be done. And they're nearly here. You need to be looked at by the medic."

Dakota shuddered. She hadn't even thought to call a fire department. On the mission field, where she'd grown up, you took care of your own emergencies when they happened. Her forehead throbbed and she touched it. "I didn't even think—how did they know?" Every thought she searched for seemed buried in mud.

Justus swept his hands in a slow stroke against her damp shoulders. "It's okay. I called them. Is there anyone else in the house?"

She shook her head. "No. I'm the only one here right now." She glanced toward the corner of the house where her office was. She couldn't quite see the extent of the damage to the front of the house in the darkness, but what she could see didn't look good. And she didn't know how she would finagle a tarp around those upthrust branches. She hadn't thought about maybe needing a saw as well.

Hopelessness begged for entrance. Her shoulders slumped. Fine, if the firemen would do that for her, that would be great. It wasn't like she was dressed for roof rescue at the moment, anyhow. Her black, ankle-length crinkled silk skirt probably wasn't the best thing to be climbing ladders in. She turned back for the garage. "Let me just grab them the tarp."

He followed her inside, but she realized he still had the flashlight when he took her arm and shone the light on a big metal toolbox. "You sit there."

"I have to—"

"Dakota, it's too late for the house. It's not too late for you. Sit."

There was an edge of something in his voice that made her follow his instructions.

"Thank you. Be right back. Don't move." He disappeared into the house.

The exasperating man had taken her light. And she hadn't even gotten the coffee she'd been looking forward to! She dropped her head onto one hand.

It only took that moment of sitting to recognize she was trembling from the top of her head to the tips of her toes. She pressed her quaking hands between her knees and winced as pain took a leisurely stroll through her wrist. She tucked her lower lip into her mouth and chose instead to cradle her arm against her chest.

She closed her eyes and saw again the tree toppled over her smashed desk. The orange sparks arcing into the darkness. The missing corner of the house.

She almost laughed as she realized that only a few minutes ago she'd been worried about a leak in the roof.

Would insurance cover something like this? Would the church hold her responsible? Was there something she could have done? Should she have insisted the trees be inspected when she took over the ministry for Marinville Assembly? She'd only been working this job on her own for two weeks. Before that she'd let LoriMay handle all that sort of thing.

Still cradling her wrist, she leaned forward and pressed her forehead into her knees.

She shuddered as she remembered Justus's question about other people. Thankfully Riley Ross was the only resident living here right now, and she'd gone with Marie to run wedding errands.

Riley. Tears threatened. Women like her were the reason it was so important to keep this place running. And as if she wasn't carrying a big enough burden trying to figure out how to keep House of Hope afloat, she had no idea how she was going to be able to help Riley. Dakota had only been working here a few weeks, and Riley was the first woman she'd ministered to who had lost so much. And LoriMay had up and quit unexpectedly only a week after Riley moved in. That had been two weeks ago.

Dakota had no experience helping a woman who'd been beaten by her boyfriend so badly that she'd lost her pregnancy of six months. She had no experience at keeping a passive expression when looking into an eye where the sclera was totally red due to the fist that had burst the vessels there. Riley's broken arm and ribs Dakota could deal with. There were doctors and prescriptions, and heaven knew she had certainly had her fair share of nursing experience. It was the wounds left on Riley's heart she was having a hard time figuring out how to heal.

A hand touched her shoulder and jolted her back to the present. Justus squatted in front of her.

As she sat up something stung her eye and she swiped at it.

Justus moved her fingers away from the area and pressed a soft cloth to her forehead. "Hold this." He guided her hand back to press the cloth in place, then squeezed her shoulder. He set the flashlight on the floor beside her, the light spilling across the concrete floor. "Stay put for a couple more minutes while I get a paramedic to look at you, alright?" He jogged toward the half-open garage door before she could even give a response.

She nodded, but when she heard the squawk of a couple radios she realized she should probably go talk to the firemen. So, as soon as he was out of sight, she stood.

Dizziness drained through her and she bumbled a couple of steps and threw her arms wide to catch her balance. But the floor seemed to tip up to meet her. Everything turned fuzzy and her fingers lost their grip on the cloth Justus had just given her. Her legs betrayed her and became useless limp ropes. She gave her head a little shake to fight the tug of gravity and blackness, but lost the battle and slumped to the floor.

Cold. The cement floor in the garage was very cold.

Chapter 2

Justus ducked out into the rain and jogged toward the paramedics who were just exiting their vehicle. "I've got one person injured," he yelled through the rain and wind. When the paramedic looked up, he could tell the man hadn't heard his exact words. Justus pointed to the garage and motioned for the man to follow, then turned and ran back toward Dakota.

As he loped up the drive, he tossed a glance at the huge tree thrusting across the roof from the backyard. A shudder quaked through him. He'd been driving down the street when he'd seen the tree give way before the wind. He was in town for Reece and Marie's wedding on Saturday, and they'd forgotten they had an appointment with the minister this evening, so had asked if he minded picking up Dakota.

He hadn't minded in the least, and in fact had headed this way a little early. He'd been looking forward to seeing her again. Probably more than he'd been willing to admit to himself until he'd seen that nasty cut on her forehead, and witnessed her determination to do all in her power to lessen the damage to the house. He was so glad someone had been here to stop her from climbing up onto that roof in her condition. The gash on her head was definitely going to need stitches and she might even have a bit of a concussion.

He ducked back under the garage door. Dakota lay sprawled on the floor, her face, illuminated by the weak beam of the flashlight, ghostly white. "Dakota!" Terror clawed through him, and he dashed to her side. Why had he left her alone? His hand trembled as he fumbled to find her pulse. And then she moaned and pushed herself partway up.

"Easy, Dakota. I think you passed out."

Even as he spoke she unsteadily tried to stand again.

"Whoa!" He lurched forward, gripped her shoulders, and guided her back onto the tool chest. Those crazy high heels she was in weren't doing her any favors. Squatting before her, he heard the paramedics enter behind them. "You're hurt worse than you realize. But the paramedics are here. Just let them have a look at you."

A guy with "Marinville Fire and Rescue" emblazoned on the front of his jumper, squatted before her with a med. kit. He pulled a small penlight from his pocket and peered into Dakota's face. "Hi there. My name is Luke. And this is my partner, Joel. We're just going to do a quick assessment to make sure you are safe, okay? What's your name?" The guy's light paused on the once-again bleeding wound on her forehead, and Justus tightened his fists and refused entrance to the images of another blood spattered woman that threatened to usurp his attention.

"D-Dakota."

Justus eased out a breath. At least she still remembered her own name. He started to back out of their way, but Dakota shot out one hand and clutched his arm. Her fingers slid over his forearm till they found his own. Her small hand trembled in his grasp. He swallowed and in that moment he wouldn't have moved for a million dollars. "I'm not going anywhere, just let them look at you."

The first paramedic continued to ask questions while the other shone his own light into her pupils, over her forehead, and then down to the wrist she held gingerly in her lap.

Justus heard air hiss between his teeth. Her arm was blue and swollen.

The paramedic named Luke kept speaking to Dakota in a calming tone, even while he pulled bandages and gauze from his kit and spouted some medical jargon to his partner. It was the words "overnight observation" that set Justus's heart to thumping so hard he was afraid the medics would hear it and turn to examining him next. His hand tightened of its own volition around Dakota's.

Lord, haven't I had enough of ambulances and hospitals for a lifetime?

Once again he forced the memories that tugged for his attention to the back of his mind and concentrated on the here and now.

Blood streaked one side of Dakota's hair, turning the long blonde tresses into a dark, matted clump. Even though a white bandage now compressed the wound, he could see blood already seeping through it. As the medic lifted her arm to examine it more carefully, she tucked her lower lip into her mouth and scrunched her eyes closed.

His stomach bucked. He hated that he couldn't save her from the pain.

The sound of firefighters clomping through the yard and yelling to one another rose and fell with the force of the wind.

Justus dropped his head down, staring at the blackness between his knees. The flash of another night so similar to this would no longer be abated. A night with so much more blood. So much more tragedy. So much more evil. A night filled with police and a manhunt for Treyvon McAllister, a boy-not-quite-turned-man who had so much of his life left ahead of him, but so much rage filling his heart.

He clenched his jaw and wrenched himself back to the present in time to hear...

"Would you like your boyfriend to accompany you on the ride to the hospital?"

Dakota's gaze flashed to his, her eyes widening. "No, I'm fine. I can get myself there."

The medic shifted in an uneasy way that raised

Justus's concern several notches. "I'd really like to encourage you to ride in the ambulance. We'd like to stabilize your arm a little better, and keep a careful watch on your head wound there." The man tilted her a smile that tightened something inside of Justus. "Riding with us won't be so bad. Joel might even tell you a few jokes along the way." The man chuckled, and despite Justus's annoyance over the slight flirtation, he appreciated the guy's attempt to lighten the situation.

Both medics had eyed the structure overhead a few times and he knew they were considering the soundness of the building, since the other end had been smashed by the tree.

Justus didn't bother correcting their misperception over his relationship with Dakota. He wouldn't abandon her for anything, but he was going to need his wheels once he got to the hospital. "You should ride in the ambulance. I can't have you getting blood all over the inside of my Z3." He winked at her. "Will you be okay if I follow right behind you to the hospital?"

"O-of course."

The paramedics both scowled like he was the lowest form of humanity.

But it wasn't them who changed his mind. It was the disappointment he saw flash through Dakota's eyes. He tilted his head and squeezed her fingers gently. "Never mind. I'll just leave my car here and ride with you."

"No. It's alright. You don't have to." A frown

pinched her brow.

"It will be fine. I'll just have Jalen drive it over for me later."

"Jalen?"

He brushed off her question. Jalen had worked with him for seven of the eight years he'd been at Deschutes Rejuvenation. And since Reece had known them both during his time working there, Jalen was also one of the groomsmen. The fact that the man was probably here more to talk him out of quitting his job than to be in the wedding didn't need to be mentioned right now. "Let's just get you to the hospital, okay?"

"Wait, what about the hole in the roof? The flooring will be ruined if we don't cover it."

Justus almost chuckled at her persistent concern over the crazy tarp. Instead, he touched her shoulder. "Let's just worry about you first. Besides, a single tarp isn't going to be able to cover that hole out there."

She swallowed. "It's just...I'm responsible."

A long damp strand of hair had fallen over her eyes, and he tucked it behind her ear, stirred by her distress. "I know. But there's nothing you can do about a tree falling on the house. Right now the best thing you can do is to get yourself better. You can deal with the damages later." He gently prodded her to her feet.

The paramedics rolled a gurney near her and helped her climb onto it. And as Justus followed her into the back of the ambulance he cast one more glance toward the house. He swallowed at the sight of the huge tree and the caved-in end of the house. Things could have been worse. So much worse.

Dakota woke to weak rays of sunshine and a dusky hospital room. Her brow furrowed. What was she doing here? She rolled her head toward the sound of a cart trundling by in the hallway, and pain sprang up from every corner of her mind. Her eyes fell shut and a low moan escaped.

A rustle of movement sounded on the other side of her bed and despite the throbbing she forced her neck to turn toward it and squinted a peek. The motion was at least tolerable this time.

Justus Teague, looking like he'd just woken up, sat on the front lip of a leather chair with wooden arms that couldn't have been comfortable to sleep in. He scrubbed fingers back through his blond curls, standing them all on end at protruding angles, and then met her gaze with a sleepy one of his own. "How are you feeling?"

Confusion plucked at her. She scrunched her eyes closed and tried to remember how she came to be here. It was only a moment before everything came back to her in a rush. She focused on Justus again, choosing to ignore his question because somehow she thought he might overreact to the fact that her head felt like it could possibly split open at any second. "Thank you for riding with me to the hospital." A flash of memory – her clutching his hand – pressed her lips closed in embarrassment. She averted her gaze.

He stood and lifted a cup with a straw to her lips. "Not a problem. I'm just glad I was there to help."

She realized how thirsty she really was, and that her voice had sounded dry and parched a moment ago. She guzzled like a dying woman at a desert water hole, then sank back against the pillows and sighed. "Thanks."

He tipped her a nod.

Pain pulsed through her skull again. "Do you think they might have some Tylenol I could take?"

Something tightened his features and he strode toward the door. "I'll get you a nurse."

He was back only moments later, a nurse bustling on his heels. "Your man here says you're hurting? Where is your pain, hon?"

Her man? Dakota didn't look toward Justus who was already back in his chair on the other side of the bed, but she would have loved to see the expression on his face over that misperception. Realizing she'd left the nurse waiting for her answer, she responded quickly, "My head."

"Well, that's to be expected considering the blow you took last night. Anywhere else?"

Dakota slowly assessed the other regions of her body and informed the nurse of a slight twinge in her left ankle and a larger one in her right arm.

"Also to be expected since your x-rays and scans

revealed a fracture of your arm and a sprain to your ankle."

Dakota nearly groaned. How was she supposed to walk down the aisle for Marie's wedding in less than a week if she had a sprained ankle? She didn't even remember them doing any scans.

The nurse was still talking. "The good news is, you don't appear to have anything more than a super mild concussion. So you'll probably get to go home here after a bit. First let's get you some breakfast and I'll put a little pain killer into your IV line." The nurse hastened back in the direction she'd come from.

Dakota didn't care about breakfast, but killing the gremlins that were kicking the inside of her skull sounded heavenly. She hoped that by "a little" the nurse meant at least a truckload of some painkiller that ended in "ine," or maybe a cocktail of several of them. Her eyes dropped closed until she remembered Justus was still here. She glanced over to find him, elbows propped against his knees and one cheek resting on clasped hands, studying her. Weariness draped his features, and the blond stubble he normally wore trimmed close and carefully groomed, looked a little thicker than normal.

"Have you been here all night?"

He nodded.

"I'm surprised they let you stay."

A grin transformed the tired lines of his face. "Let's just say it took a little bit of charm and a whole lot of persistence."

She offered him a weary smile. "Thanks for being here, but you don't have to stay. Go home and get some rest."

Humor tucked around the edges of his eyes. "I can't have all these nice hospital staff thinking I'm the worst boyfriend in the world."

She laughed, then, as shards of fire shot through her head, gasped and stiffened.

Justus was standing by her side in an instant. "Sorry. What can I do?"

She eased out a breath and wrinkled her nose at him. "Don't make me laugh. At least not till a few minutes after she gets back with that painkiller."

He touched her shoulder, his face serious. "You got it."

His total seriousness almost made her laugh again. She opened her mouth to tease him about it, but just then Marie and Reece knocked at the open door. She changed her intended words. "Hi, you two. Come in."

They stepped into the room, followed by Riley and a dark haired Hispanic looking man she'd never seen before.

Marie rushed to her side. "Dakota! I can't believe it! I hardly slept last night, I was so worried about you. Are you going to be okay?" She leaned over the bed and gave Dakota a gentle hug.

Dakota patted her back. "I'm going to be fine. Where's my munchkin?"

"Darlene is watching her this morning."

Reece's mom seemed to have come around one hundred percent in her opinion of Marie over the last few months. Dakota was glad about that. Especially for Marie's four-year-old daughter Alyssa's sake.

She moved on to a more pressing matter. "I just hope this isn't going to ruin the wedding."

Marie waved away her concern and rejoined Reece at the foot of the bed. "Our wedding should be the least of your worries. I can't believe a tree fell on House of Hope!"

"Crazy, huh?" Dakota tried not to wince when Marie rested one hand on her sprained ankle at the end of the bed.

Reece pushed his ever present cowboy hat back on his head and folded his arms. "So what do you hear about when you get to make your escape?"

Dakota offered a thin smile, feeling her energy already beginning to flag. "The jailer said I'm up for parole this morning sometime."

Just then the nurse stepped back in carrying a breakfast tray. "Well, look at you, Miss Center of the Party." She offered Dakota a wink as she set the tray on the rolling bedside table. She pulled a syringe from her coat pocket and reached for Dakota's IV port. "A few painkillers and you'll be up and dancing with one of these handsome guys in no time."

Everyone chuckled and Dakota couldn't remember being happier to see a syringe full of drugs in her life.

A warm hand settled against her shoulder. "You alright?"

She forced herself to meet Justus's concerned scrutiny. "I'm fine."

He stepped over to his chair and pulled his black leather jacket from the back. "Tell you what. We'll all let you eat and we'll run grab a bite ourselves. Then I'll be here again about ten to see if you've been released and to give you a ride, alright?"

As nice as it would be to simply agree and let him control the situation, he'd already done more than enough. Besides, she knew from talking to Reece that Justus had done time. How safe could it be to be alone with him, no matter how secure he made her feel?

She arched her brows at Marie. "Actually, if Marie's done with my car I can just drive myself?"

Marie darted Reece a look, then Justus. Neither man seemed to want to meet Dakota's gaze. But there was compassion in Marie's eyes when she looked at her. "Um... We sort of don't want you driving yourself anywhere, at least for a couple days.

Dakota's brows shot up. "We?"

Marie winced and swung a finger to Reece, then on to Justus, and back to herself with a tiny nod.

"Guys! I'm a big girl who bumped her head. I'm perfectly capable of taking care of myself and don't need you babying me."

Justus cleared his throat. "You have a slight concussion. A broken arm. And a sprained ankle. Be reasonable." Without giving her another chance to protest he turned to the nurse. "So will ten be a good time to check back?"

The nurse agreed that the timing should be about right and adjusted Dakota's table. "You just eat when you are ready, okay?" With that she made her way from the room.

Despite her grumpiness over their three-way conspiracy, Dakota liked the feeling of being taken care of – especially by Justus – just a little too much. How was it she could so enjoy the company of an ex-con? Her parents were always thousands of miles away on another continent, and she'd simply adjusted to doing for herself, she supposed. But now...she met Justus's warm blue eyes filled with concern and her heart sped up in a way it hadn't since Jason. *Jason.* There were so many reasons why she needed to avoid a relationship right now – especially with a guy like Justus – and she suddenly felt a little desperate to avoid the impending alone-time with him.

She tore her gaze from his and settled it on Marie. "Marie, Justus has already done more than enough. Couldn't you pick me up then?"

Marie shook her head. "Sorry, Reece and I have to run to Portland today to grab the supplies for the reception. But Justus has already offered to be your chauffeur for the next couple of days. And Riley's going to drive your car out to Serenity Shores for you so it will be there when you are able to drive yourself again."

The next couple of days? Her pulse picked up at just the thought, and she hoped no one was studying the display on the monitor next to her bed too closely.

Do not make the same mistake twice!

Her gaze flicked to Justus once more. What had sent him to jail?

Jail time wasn't the only drawback to the man. She distinctly remembered his death-trap of a red motorbike. She lifted one brow at Justus, unable to hide her pique. "You going to make me ride behind you on your motorbike?" Her chest tightened at just the thought. She'd sooner walk home than straddle a bike ever again.

But he only shook his head. "Left my bike back home this time. Brought my car, instead." He tipped his head at the Hispanic man. "Jalen there protested over having to ride with the wind in his face the whole way here. Good thing too, I guess."

Jalen, standing quietly, arms folded, smirked and shook his head over the obvious misrepresentation, but tilted her a nod of greeting.

She wiggled her fingers in return, since moving her head still hurt like crazy. "So Riley, you aren't going to Portland with Marie and Reece today?"

Riley shook her head.

Dakota studied the woman. Her face was as impassive and unreadable as usual. Dakota sighed. At least she didn't have to worry about Riley's safety from her ex-boyfriend since he'd driven his car off the coastal highway and been killed instantly the night he'd last beaten her up. Even so, Dakota didn't want Riley to be alone. She had so many emotions roiling through her right now.

Dakota pressed her lips together, not wanting to make her feel self-conscious in front of all those in the room, but not wanting to leave her to be on her own all day either.

Jalen saved her from the dilemma. "If Riley doesn't mind, Marie asked me to deejay for the wedding reception on Saturday, and I could use some help checking out the church's equipment and doing some sound tests."

Dakota liked the man already. She looked at Riley and waited for her reply.

Riley shrugged and gave a tiny nod.

And Dakota offered Jalen a smile of thanks.

He lifted his chin in a quick nod to indicate it was no big deal, shoved his hands deep into his pockets, and scuffed one toe at the floor.

Marie broke the awkward silence that settled. "Thanks for letting me use your car yesterday. That was a big help.

"You're welcome. But I'm not happy that you guys are all ganging up on me." Dakota stuck her tongue out at Marie.

Marie only chuckled. "I'm sure you'll get over it." But her gaze traveled to Riley, who stood quietly, her focus sweeping each aspect of the room as if to memorize the space.

Dakota was suddenly hit with a concerning thought. "Riley, where did you sleep last night? Are you okay?"

Riley's attention zoomed to her, then flicked to Marie, but she didn't speak, only nodded and tucked a strand of her straight red-blonde hair behind one ear.

Jalen looked down and kicked at something on a tile near his feet, his jaw jutting off to one side.

Marie hastened to speak for her. "Riley stayed with Alyssa and me last night, and she's welcome to stay until we get another place figured out...."

Marie's words trailed away, and Dakota knew the implication. She was welcome to stay until something else was figured out or until Marie's lease ran out at the end of the week when she and her daughter would move into Serenity Shores with Reece.

Which brought to mind another thought for Dakota. *She* didn't have a place to stay either. Where was she going to go when she left here today? The fire department had condemned House of Hope, and all of Dakota's and Riley's belongings were in there.

Reece seemed to be able to read her thoughts. "Listen, with the wedding coming up, we didn't book any guests at Serenity Shores for about three weeks. We'll have plenty of room for you two plus all the wedding guests. So no need to worry about where you're going to stay."

Relief rushed through Dakota. But it was Riley who concerned her. She offered the woman a smile. "Sounds good to me. What about you?"

Riley shrugged and nodded, still offering no word or flicker of emotion.

Lord, help me to reach her. "Good. It's settled then. Thank you, Reece. That lifts a big weight from my mind."

Everyone started to head for the door then, but Dakota needed to know the truth about Justus before any more time passed. "Reece? Could I talk to you for a minute?" Thankfully everyone seemed to get the hint that she wanted a word alone with him, and Reece lingered while everyone else left the room.

She picked at the blanket, trying to determine the best way to ask her question but no diplomatic turn of phrase came to mind. Finally she just plunged in. "Listen, I know he's your friend...but didn't you tell me Justus served time? Should I be careful about being alone with him?"

Reece actually chuckled. "No. Not at all. There's no one you should trust more than Justus. He did serve time, but that's his story to tell, and I'm sure he'll get around to telling you someday. But you don't need to question your safety with him, and trust me when I say he's a different man now, and there's no need for concern."

Dakota chewed the inside of her lip. No need for concern except she might lose her heart to the guy! "Okay. If you're sure. Thanks. Sorry. I—" She waved a hand, unsure what else she wanted to say.

"I'm totally sure. Don't worry about it. You're in good hands with him, I promise you. You good now?"

"Yes. Thanks."

He nodded and stepped out into the hall.

Dakota released a soft sigh as she lifted the lid from her plate of food. All she really wanted to do was sleep, but she'd force a few bites down first.

And try not to think about the enigma that composed Justus Teague. How did an ex-con engender such loyalty from his friends? When it came down to tallying pros and cons for potential men to date, "previous prisoner" was definitely a big mark in the "con" column. Not to mention his obvious thrill seeking, daredevil, need-for-speed side. But in the "pro" column she'd have to mark down a man who'd slept the whole night in an uncomfortable chair for a woman he barely knew just so she'd have someone close by in case she needed anything. And those blue eyes that probed every nuance of her face with a soft compassion that drew her like a warm fire on a cold day. Definitely those.

She gave up trying to understand the complex swirl of emotions spinning through her, pushed the food tray away, and sank against the softness of the pillows.

Unfortunately, exhausted as she was, sleep remained elusive. First the doctor came in on his morning rounds. He double checked all her injuries, assessed the response of her pupils to light, listened to her heartbeat, and checked her blood pressure and pulse. He offered her a gentle smile.

"You are lucky, young lady. Your injuries could have been much worse."

Dakota swallowed. "Yeah, I think God was watching out for me. I was sitting at my desk right where the tree fell only moments before it happened."

The doctor gave a little whistle. "Well, however you were spared, you've managed to escape with only a slight concussion, a few stitches, and injuries that will heal within a few weeks." He jotted something in her chart. "I'll write up the order for your discharge and you are free to leave as soon as the nurse brings by your prescription for pain killers. The stitches on your forehead will dissolve on their own, and I'll take a look at them at our appointment next week." He glanced at her chart again. "I see you've had malaria. Had any flare-ups recently?"

"No." She shook her head.

"Good. Well..." He stood. "We'll get you out of here as soon as we can."

Dakota figured she'd better hear the bad news straight from the horse's mouth if it was going to be bad news, so she took a breath and asked, "I'm in a wedding on Saturday. Will I be able to walk by then?"

To her surprise the doctor nodded. "Your sprain isn't too severe. I'd like you to wear this ankle boot until Friday, but I think it will be okay to remove it and participate in the wedding on Saturday. Just listen to your body. Too much pain means it's not ready yet. Any other questions?"

Relieved at the answer, Dakota shook her head.

"Alright then..." The doctor stood and shook her hand. "Sometimes a trauma like this, especially one that results in exhaustion, can cause a relapse of the malaria. So please take it easy over the next few days for sure and give yourself lots of rest."

She smiled. "The way I feel now, my body will be demanding that from me."

"Good. Listen to it!"

Dakota had just once more settled into her pillow to hopefully find a few moments of the doctor's last prescription, when a knock at the open door revealed Pastor Mark poking his head inside.

"Hi Pastor." She waved him in. "Thanks for coming by."

Pastor shook his head as he approached. "I'm so glad you are okay!"

Dakota made a face of regret. "I'm really sorry about House of Hope. Is it going to be fixable?"

Pastor Mark held out a hand to reassure her. "Don't you worry about a thing. The house is insured, and just a year ago the insurance company had a man come out and check over those trees at our request and expense. He gave them the all-clear to remain. So I have every confidence that the damage to the house will be fully covered. The most important thing is that you're okay."

Relief washed through Dakota so palpably she realized how much her concern had been weighing on her. "I'm so glad to hear that."

He folded his arms. "Of course House of Hope has been condemned until repairs can be made. Police Chief Tom Hansen said to just give them a call when you want to get some of your things and he'd have an officer meet you on the scene. Riley said anytime would work for her."

"Okay, thanks for letting me know."

Pastor looked chagrinned then. "I saw I missed a call from you last night." He winced. "I really hope you weren't trying to get a hold of me after the tree fell?"

She rushed to reassure him. "Oh no! That was before. I wanted to talk to you about the books. There are some things not seeming to add up in the accounting for House of Hope."

"Oh? What?"

"Well, to me it looks like some money may be missing somewhere."

Pastor Mark's eyebrows peaked. "That doesn't sound good."

"Is there a time I could come by and we could look at the numbers together? You might know something I don't with regards to it."

"Sure." Pastor pulled out his phone and consulted his calendar. "How about next week some time? After you have the wedding out of the way? Say Tuesday afternoon about two thirty In the meantime I'll take a look at the account myself to see if I can find the discrepancy."

Dakota smiled, relieved to know she could talk to him about it. "That sounds good."

Pastor stayed and prayed with her and visited until Justus stepped back into the room. Pastor Mark stood from where he'd seated himself in the room's chair.

Freshly showered and groomed, the sight of Justus, and the sweep of his swimming-pool-blue eyes, stole all the moisture from Dakota's mouth. "Pastor Mark." The words rasped and she cleared her throat and started again. "Pastor Mark, this is Justus Teague. He's a good friend of Reece's and here for the wedding. Justus, this is our pastor, Mark Rolland."

Justus nodded and stepped forward to shake the man's hand.

"Well." Pastor Mark turned back to her after greeting Justus. "I'd better be going. Mrs. Murton is in here too. Got struck by a branch when she was out walking her Pomeranian last night."

A surge of sorrow and guilt shot through Dakota at the mention of old Mrs. Murton. But Pastor Mark wouldn't know that a good deal of the woman's loneliness was Dakota's fault. Mrs. Murton wouldn't know either, for that matter. Dakota forced her lips to form words. "Oh, I'm so sorry to hear that. Is she going to be alright?"

Pastor nodded. "Yes, she just cut her arm pretty good, and they wanted to keep an eye on her blood pressure overnight. But her call this morning said it was stabilizing. Anyhow, just say a prayer for her, if you would."

"I will. And I'll stop by to say hello to her on my

way out. What room is she in?"

"Just down the hall in room 307. Thanks for praying. I know she'll do the same for you." He lifted a hand of farewell, then paused. "I'm assuming you have all the help you need, and a place to stay?"

Dakota nodded. "Yes. Thank you."

"Good. Well, you just let us know if you need anything, alright? And I'll be seeing you soon."

After she signed discharge papers and received her prescription, Dakota fought her casted arm and booted foot to dress in the same clothes she'd worn the day before, while Justus waited in the hallway. The sleeve of her blouse wouldn't fit over the cast and she had to tear it to get it on, and the Velcro on the boot snagged her skirt several times before she managed to smooth it into place. Finally she sank down onto her bed to slip on one shoe. Why, oh why had she chosen yesterday to wear the mint shoes, she wondered as she thrust her good foot into one of the high heels and tossed the other shoe into the small bag the hospital had given her.

Task number one accomplished, she eyed the crutches leaning next to her with some trepidation. Task number two was to get herself to Justus's car without making too much of a fool of herself.

But how was she to use the crutches when one of her arms was casted and hurt every time she moved it? "Lots of weight on the armpit and you'll just have to use your hand to swing the crutch forward. Come on. You can do this."

Her little pep talk didn't make her feel much better, but she forced herself into motion and stood. She balanced precariously on her heel and tucked the crutches under her arms, then fumbled to loop the canvas bag's handles over her head.

Thankfully, the door to her room was a sliding one that was easy to open.

Justus waited for her, one shoulder planted into the hallway wall and arms folded. His black leather jacket stretched tight over his broad shoulders and looked way too good. It made her self-conscious of her messy hospital hair, lack of a shower, and probably barely-there-smudges of makeup.

He stood when he saw her. "Ready?" His gaze swept down and paused on her shoe before rebounding to her eyes. His lips twitched. "I better find you a wheelchair."

"No. No. I'll be fine. I have to get the hang of this sometime. Might as well start now."

She awkwardly swept the crutches forward and did her best to ignore the throbbing in her arm. The hospital bag swung out and then flopped back against her belly like lead weight on a plumb line.

Justus stepped up right in front of her and relieved her of the bag. He didn't move back but stayed where he was, looking down into her face. "What's your middle name?"

Her brow puckered. "Jean. Why?"

"Jean's so normal. I figured it might be stubborn or obstinate or something like that." He winked.

She swung her good hand to smack him, but he

just laughed and ducked away. "Come on gimpy. The elevator's at the end of the hall. We'd better get started if we want to make it home by tonight."

"I just want to swing by Mrs. Murton's room on the way out."

But there was no need to search out her room, because a grey haired woman in a hospital gown was coming toward them from the other end of the hallway. She smiled and waved.

Dakota's heart filled with love and dread all at once – just like it did each time she saw the woman. "Hi Mrs. Murton."

"Dakota, dear! It's so nice to see you! Well, not here necessarily, but you know what I mean." She smiled.

"It's good to see you too. Are you going to be okay?"

Mrs. Murton waved away her concern. "Pastor Mark told me about the house. I couldn't believe it." She reached out and squeezed Dakota's good hand where it rested on the padding of the crutch's handle.

"Yes. Pretty crazy. But the worst that happened is my broken arm."

"Bones do heal, I suppose. I'm very glad you weren't hurt worse." The truth of her words shone in the older woman's expression.

And threatened to bring Dakota to tears. "Thank you." How she wished the past could be different.

Mrs. Murton's soft blue eyes angled toward Justus, and a glimmer of curiosity and interest registered. "Who's this nice looking man, dear?" The tone of her voice said the elderly widow would be the highest bidder if Justus were on an auction block.

"Uh..." Dakota looked down and scrubbed at a mark on the floor with the tip of one crutch. That nurse must have given her a dose of some crazy drug, because she was suddenly experiencing a hot flash she felt sure could be seen on satellite from space. "This is Justus Teague. He's in town to be in Reece and Marie's wedding on Saturday."

"Oh, he knows the Cahill boy?" Mrs. Murton assessed him from the top of his blond head to his black leather work boots and back. "Well, he must be alright then." She offered Justus a smile that he returned with an offered hand.

"Nice to meet you. Mrs. Murton, is it?"

"Yes, dear." She accepted his handshake into a two handed grip and leaned close to speak right into his face. "You take care of my Dakota, you hear? No hanky panky. She's a good girl."

Justus blinked. "Yes, ma'am." He glanced over and grinned at her.

Somewhere in a scientific lab, there were meltdown-danger sirens sounding a warning because of the heat flash surging through her. Dakota wished for a fan. Or maybe just a straight-up ice bath. Her cheeks felt like they might be on fire.

And Mrs. Murton only made it worse by turning to her and pinching her chin. "I'm glad you have found someone else. Jason would be happy for you. Well…" She stepped to one side and continued down the corridor, waving to them over her shoulder. "If I ever want them to let me out of here I have to prove that I'm capable of walking this hallway without my blood pressure going through the roof. So goodbye for now. I'll see you at the wedding, I presume."

"Bye." Dakota willed away the guilt the mention of Jason brought and glanced at Justus, half expecting to be grilled about who he was.

But all he said was, "She seems like a lady who cares for you very much."

Dakota forced herself to head for the stairs. "Yes. She does."

Despite her insistence that she would be just fine walking to the car, Dakota had never felt more thankful than when she sank into the warm leather seat of Justus's BMW Z3. Her leg trembled from exhaustion, and her arm was hurting like nobody's business.

She relaxed into the seat and scanned the interior as she waited for him to stow her crutches in the trunk and get in on his side. Burl wood accents glowed golden against the backdrop of the black leather interior. The heated seat button beckoned, and she clicked it to the "high" position, already feeling a bit of a chill after leaving the warm blankets of her hospital bed. Hopefully it wouldn't take too long to heat up after he turned on the car.

She scanned the sky outside, amazed at the beautiful day. No one experiencing today would ever think that just a few hours ago the wind had been howling so ferociously that it had knocked a tree over on her house. Cloudless blue skies. Slight breezes. Sunshine. Weak December sunshine, but sunshine nevertheless. It was like a new blank page. A new opportunity. Maybe something better would come from all of this? She sighed.

Okay, Lord. We'll rebuild. One day at a time. One life at a time. Give me the strength I'm going to need to get the job done.

Justus sank into the driver's seat and glanced over at her. Once again she was taken aback by the azure blue of his eyes. She tipped her head against the headrest and worked her teeth over her lower lip. *Cons, Dakota, cons! He's an adrenaline junky who spent time in jail for who knows what. And just look at this car. It might have four wheels, but if ever a car revealed something about the personality of its driver, this is it.* No. He was definitely not the type of man she wanted to get into a relationship with again, no matter how much her fingers itched to reach out and touch the prickly, thick five o'clock shadow on his cheeks.

His gaze roamed her features, lingering on the spot where she knew a line of black stitches etched the skin near her temple. "You don't look like you got much rest this morning."

She wrinkled her nose and made a face, taking a fortifying breath at the reminder of just how terrible she must look. "Nor a shower. Nor clean clothes. I'm a mess. Do you think we could stop by the house on our way out to Serenity Shores Bed and Breakfast and grab some of my things? I just have to call, and they'll have an officer meet us there. Riley said anytime was fine with her."

He looked dubious. "Why don't you let me run you out to Reece's place and then I can come back in and grab some stuff for you?"

The thought of having Justus fetching her clean underwear burned embarrassment across the back of her neck. "Um, I'd rather just stop there myself, if you don't mind. It's on the way and will only take a few minutes."

He sighed. "Like I said...stubborn runs thick in your veins."

She couldn't help a giggle. "My daddy used to say they put my picture in the dictionary next to 'pigheaded.'" The fingernails of her good hand bit into her palm. What had made her simper like a teenager in love for the first time? It must be the exhaustion making her giddy.

Humor softened the concern tightening his features. "I'll have to remember that." He sat back and inserted the key. "Make the call."

She eased out a breath of satisfaction. "Thank you."

He grinned. "I bet you didn't often have to fight very hard to get your way either, did you?"

She pursed her lips and thought back to her childhood on the mission field in Africa. "Guess not too often. Why?"

He laughed outright then. "Because any man looking into your big blue eyes would sooner melt into a puddle than deny you a thing."

Alarm shot through her. However she forced a smile and when he looked over and offered a crooked grin, batted her eyelashes with great fanfare.

But as he pulled out of the hospital parking lot she turned her focus to the scenery out her passenger window and buttoned down all the heartache that had just threatened to explode all over everything. No way could Justus know the memories those few words had jostled loose. Neither could he know it had been her begging and pleading that had led Jason straight to his own death.

And almost to hers.

Chapter 3

Justus berated himself as he pulled the car to a stop in front of House of Hope. He didn't know what he'd said, but he'd obviously said something wrong, because the normally talkative Dakota hadn't said a word since they left the hospital parking lot.

Now she clipped out, "The officer should be here any minute."

He glanced over at her, but she hadn't budged, so he peered out the windows toward the house, not wanting to push her by asking what the matter was.

Caution tape cordoned off most of the yard. And it looked like a crew had been by to remove the tree, based on the lack of protruding branches and the huge swath of plastic sheeting tied over the gaping hole in the roof.

She clicked her fingernails against the cast on her right arm, tapping out a rhythm reminiscent of the "William Tell Overture."

Finally he reached over and stilled her nervousness.

Her gaze leapt to his.

He tried not to notice how good her slender fingers felt beneath his own, because a relationship with a woman, no matter how beautiful and enticing she might be, was the last thing he needed in his life right now with the mess it was in – even if he hadn't been able to think of much for the past two weeks other than how he was looking forward to seeing her. "I'm sorry."

A furrow ticked her brow. "For what?"

He released her hand and eased back to his own side of the vehicle. "I'm not sure. I think I said something that upset you."

She shook her head. "It wasn't you...." Her words trailed off, and her focus blurred against the dashboard for so long he was just about to reach over and still her fingers once again when she seemed to shake off her melancholy. "Well, we aren't going to get my stuff just sitting out here, are we?" She reached for her door handle.

Justus touched her shoulder. "Let me get your crutches. Sit tight." He wanted to pry for more details, wanted to know what thoughts churned the cogs behind those beautiful blue eyes of hers. But he let her have her space and climbed from the car.

Bringing the crutches to her door, he waited till she'd swung her legs out and then reached in to grasp her good arm and pull her to her one good leg. When she was standing at full height her head came to just under his chin, despite her crazy shoes. She clutched his arm in a fireman hold to catch her balance and looked up. And he felt the power of her azure scrutiny all the way to his toes. For a moment he forgot the crutches clutched in his free hand. Her forearm was warm and smooth beneath his hand, and before he realized what he was doing he'd stroked his thumb several times across the inner pulse point at her elbow.

Dakota swallowed visibly. "Justus—" She broke off whatever she'd been about to say and tore her gaze from his, then reached for the crutches. "Why were you here last night? I hadn't even heard you were back in town, yet."

He gave himself a mental shake and stepped back, but not so far that he wouldn't be near enough to catch her if she lost her balance. "I came a few days early, and Reece and Marie had an appointment with the pastor, so they asked me to come get you at six."

She angled him a look. "You were there just after five."

He shrugged and considered his response. He might as well test the waters a little. Forbidden though they might be. "Maybe I was looking forward to seeing you."

"Right!"

"What? You don't believe me?"

She tilted her head. Narrowed her humor-filled eyes. "You could have gotten my number from Reece at any time and gotten in touch over the past several months. But you didn't. And I'm supposed to believe you came by early because you wanted to see me?"

That was true enough. Did he dare admit to her the number of times he'd almost asked Reece for her contact information? He folded his arms and leaned into his heels. "Maybe I'm shy."

She laughed and shook her head. "No."

He couldn't resist the smile that begged for release. "Maybe I was worried you wouldn't take my call or respond to a text."

"You should have been worried about that. Because I for sure would have ignored you, just so you know." There was a hint of sass in the look she gave him. But as she tried to swing a step forward her ankle boot caught against the crutch, and with her other foot in the totally impractical high heeled shoe she started to topple.

He lunged forward and grabbed her waist, getting his shin clipped by a crutch for his trouble. He forced his lips to stretch into what he hoped she would mistake for a grin and looked down at her, arching one brow.

Her eyes were a bit wide, but other than that, she seemed fine. "Thanks." She wrinkled her nose sheepishly.

He gave her a little space and moved the conversation back on track. "Maybe my life has been so complicated lately that there hasn't been room in it for a relationship." He nearly winced. He hadn't meant to strike so close to the truth.

She frowned and seemed to ponder his words as she adjusted the crutches.

He waited till she had them settled firmly under her arms. "You good?"

She leaned into them and nodded.

He gave her a little more space, still keeping a close eye on her in case she needed help again.

"Complicated I can understand. Which brings me to what I wanted to say…"

He waited quietly, not quite sure what to feel. It might be a relief if she told him she wasn't interested. Would certainly make things easier and less complicated.

"I wanted to say thanks again for staying with me last night. I wasn't really feeling like myself, and I hope I didn't make you feel obligated in any way."

He stepped out of her path and folded his arms. He tightened his jaw, a little bit terrified over just how much it had meant to have her to reach out for him last night. He spent so much of his life being rejected by the boys he was trying to help; being let down – even horrified – by their actions. To have someone actually reach to him. Need him. Want him nearby. Well that feeling was quite unlike any other. But he couldn't tell her all of that, because that would just sound loony. So what he said was, "I stayed because I wanted to."

"Well… thank you. It's just…I remember grabbing your hand and…" Her cheeks turned a pretty shade that brought to mind strawberries and cream on a warm summer day. She crutched a couple steps and glanced down the street, muttering something to herself that he didn't quite catch.

But it reminded him of the first time he'd met her. The time she'd been talking to herself and he'd overheard her call him "calendar worthy." He grinned at that. And just then she turned and caught his humor.

Her cheeks brightened another shade. "I'm talking to myself again, huh?"

He gave in to the urge to tease her a little. "It's okay. I've learned some enlightening things while listening to you talk to yourself."

She laughed uneasily. "Justus, I know I said..."

Her expression begged for his help, but he was having too much fun with this to let her off easy. "You said what?"

She squinched her nose at him. "You know exactly what I said, but I want you to know, that just because I said you were...nice looking, doesn't mean I can be in a relationship right now." The sincere set of her gaze said she hoped her gentle rejection would be taken seriously.

He eased out a breath. The words had hurt a lot more than he'd expected them to. But this was good. And what else was he to expect? He felt pretty sure Reece had told her about his time behind bars. A couple times he'd seen a hint of curiosity mixed with fear on her face as she studied him. He gave himself a mental shake. Yes, this was better. "I'm actually glad you said that, because while I also find you attractive, I wasn't really kidding about what I said. My life is in a bit of chaos right now and it's not really a good time for me to be in a relationship."

Dakota eased out a silent breath. See? She'd known he was only being a nice guy who didn't want to hurt her feelings. And what she'd said was mostly true. She really *couldn't* be in a relationship right now. But it wouldn't have hurt her feelings much if he'd at least pretended like he'd wanted a bit more than friendship from her. At least he'd said she was attractive. She'd have to live with that, she supposed.

His brows arched as he waited for her reply.

She pursed her lips and forced herself to nod like all was as she'd hoped. "Good. So...friends?" She leaned in to her crutches and held out her casted hand to him.

He stepped close and gently gripped the fingers protruding from the end of the plaster. "Friends." His touch was more like a soft caress, as though he feared he might hurt her if he squeezed her fingers too hard.

A zing of awareness zipped up her arm and down her spine. Oh boy. Maybe the handshake had been a mistake. She tugged to be released, but instead of letting her go he moved into her personal space, maintaining his gentle grasp. And when her gaze flew to his, he grinned. "I'm going to like being your friend, Dakota Trask."

And I'm going to be tortured to only be yours, Justus Teague.

He swept a glance toward her shoes. "As your friend can I just say for the duration of the time you are on crutches, it would probably be best to wear flat, practical shoes?" He winked.

She stretched out her leg and angled her mint suede spool heel back and forth. "What? You don't think these are the best crutching gear?"

The squad car pulled up just then and Tom Hansen stepped from the vehicle.

Justus moved back and Dakota smiled at the Police Chief. "Hi, Chief. Couldn't find anyone else to babysit me, huh?"

He chuckled. "Unfortunately, there was a lot of damage last night and all my officers are occupied elsewhere." He swung a look to Justus.

Dakota pointed the end of her crutch at him. "This is Justus Teague. Justus," she swung a gesture back toward the officer, "Chief of Police Tom Hansen."

Justus nodded and shook the man's hand.

The chief ambled up the walkway to the front door. "Riley coming?"

"She should be here any minute. I called her when we were leaving the hospital. Thanks for letting us in to get our stuff."

Tom smiled at her over his shoulder. "Sure. We can't have you ladies living without your shoe collections."

Justus's laughter floated on the wind. "That

would be a tragedy for sure!"

Dakota chuckled and felt heat sear her cheeks. "It is true. I can't wait to put on my Vans!"

Chapter 4

Friday morning, Dakota hobbled down the upper hallway at Serenity Shores, determined she was going to do something helpful for the wedding today, whether or not anyone protested. She was the maid of honor and supposed to be taking weight off of Marie, but for the past couple days no one had hardly let her lift a finger to help with anything.

Today they were all heading to the church to set up the final decorations for tomorrow's ceremony, and she was going to be there even if she had to stow away in Justus's trunk.

After they finalized the decorations, the rehearsal and dinner would take place later this evening. But first Marie and Reece had asked all their bridesmaids and groomsmen to meet with them here at Serenity Shores for a brunch. And if the smells of bacon, sausage, and green peppers wafting up the stairway were any indication, they were all in for a real treat from Darlene's kitchen this morning.

Gripping her crutches under her casted arm, and the stair rail with the other hand, Dakota hopped down the staircase on one foot. It would be a miracle if her right quad wasn't twice the size of her left before her ankle healed.

"Aunt Kota!" Marie's daughter, four-year-old Alyssa Sinclair, launched herself at Dakota's legs the minute she came off the last step. Chubby arms wrapped her in a hug, crutches and all.

Dakota stumbled a sideways step, grateful for a wall to plant her shoulder into. "Whoa there, Superwoman! You about took me out!"

"Sorry." Alyssa paused long enough to offer a sheepish smile before spinning on one heel to dash toward the dining room. "Come on! Grandma made breakfast!" she called over her rapidly disappearing shoulder.

"I'm coming. But I'm slower than you on a good day, and today's not a good day." The words were spoken to thin air, because Alyssa had already turned the corner at the end of the hallway.

Giving a little growl, she tucked the duo of speed impediments under her armpits.

"Feeling a little grumbly about our limitations are we?" Justus trotted down the stairs and paused beside her.

Even after two days of telling herself he only wanted to be her friend, her pulse still spiked every time he walked into the room. She bit back her frustration over that fact and tried not to look as grumpy as she felt. "My armpits hurt," she groused.

He tilted her a look of sympathy. "Today's the last day, right? The doctor said you are allowed to walk down the aisle tomorrow?"

She wished he'd be a little less compassionate. It would make it easier on her heart. She gave him a sour look. "Sure, I get to waddle like a penguin down the aisle at my best friend's wedding. Oh joy!"

He chuckled and scrubbed a hand over the back of his neck, studying her. "Glad to see you haven't lost your bright outlook on life."

She crinkled her nose. "I am being a brat, aren't I? I could be lying in the hospital or worse right now, and all I can think of is how frustrated I am that I can't do more to help."

His face turned serious. "I wouldn't say 'being a brat.' Just learning to be content in all circumstances, which I know isn't easy."

She sighed. "Isn't that the truth!"

He chuckled and tapped her nose. "Come on, Grumpy. The other dwarfs are waiting for us in the dining room."

"Har, har." She clunked after him down the hallway.

Justus pulled out her chair and helped her stow her crutches against the wall behind her, and when she reached for a plate, even commandeered it from her and filled it with the items she pointed out so she wouldn't have to stand on her one good leg to reach the buffet style food.

He set the plate down in front of her with a

steaming cup of coffee next to it and arched a brow as if to ask if it all looked right.

"Thank you." She gave him a smile, even though she hated not being able to fend for herself. She really ought to be more thankful for all the help he'd given her over the past few days since the storm.

"My pleasure." He filled his own plate and then sank down next to her.

With her mouth stuffed full, she witnessed him pause to bow his head before he dug into his own fare, and felt a prick of guilt. *Bad boy turned good?* She logged another mark on the pros side of her imaginary tally sheet.

She swallowed the delicious bite of stuffed green pepper and then followed his example. She hadn't been grateful for much lately, and she really had a lot to be grateful for.

She and Justus chatted amiably while they ate and others filtered into the room and filled their own plates. Dakota had been honored and a little surprised when Marie had asked her if she would be her maid of honor. She'd figured Taysia would get that distinction, but Marie explained that they had wanted Taysia and her husband Kylen, who was one of the groomsmen, to be able to walk together up the aisle, and Taysia had been perfectly happy with that decision. Riley was also a bridesmaid. Reece had chosen Justus as his best man, and Jalen, whom he had also worked with for years at Deschutes Rejuvenation, as his third groomsman.

By the time everyone gathered around the table, Dakota felt a bit like a sardine. But she loved this. She studied the occupants of the Serenity Shores dining room. Kylen and Taysia were laughing hysterically over something with Reece and Marie. Alyssa, her tongue stuck between her teeth, had her head tilted just so as she attempted to get something right in a drawing she was working on. And beside the little girl Darlene leaned in to see what she was sketching. Across the table from Dakota, Riley remained quiet, but she didn't seem as withdrawn today as she had been for the past weeks. Next to Riley, Jalen fiddled with the fork on his empty plate, a small frown pinching his brow. He was a riddle she hadn't quite figured out yet. He would laugh and joke when Riley wasn't in the room, but the minute she walked in, it was like an emotional blanket dropped over him.

Stuffed too full to finish everything on her plate, Dakota pushed back from the table as an expectant silence finally settled. Dakota turned to look at Reece and Marie along with everyone else, wondering why they'd been called here.

Marie gave Reece an excited little glance and then rubbed her hands together as she scanned them all. Dakota felt the bottom begin to drop out of her stomach. What had Marie schemed up for them?

"Okay, everyone, Reece and I have something we'd like to ask of all of you." Her attention honed in on Dakota. "We'd wanted to do this, and then when Dakota was injured we weren't sure we could pull it off, but now that she's for sure going to be able to walk tomorrow, we'd like to try."

Try what? Dakota liked the sound of this less and less. Maybe her foot would have a tragic setback tomorrow.

"So what we'd like is for each of you to join us on the dance floor for our first dance, but we want to end the dance with a little bit of a choreographed routine."

Dakota's gaze darted to Justus's, only to find he was already looking at her, brows raised, humor dancing in his eyes. Dakota snapped her lips together to keep her jaw from dropping open.

Marie held up her hands. "I know. I know. It sounds complicated, but I promise it is not going to be too complex. We are going to make it super easy on all of you and we even have time planned to practice today at the rehearsal."

Dakota swallowed, but there was no moisture in her mouth whatsoever. She snatched up her coffee mug and took a big swig that burned all the way down.

They wanted her to *dance?* Did they know she'd grown up mostly on the mission field and hadn't been allowed to dance one day in her life? She didn't know the difference between a waltz and a disco, for crying in her coffee. Yes, a good cry would be so comforting right about now. No one would fault her for indulging in a nice prescription of tears and caffeine, would they?

Justus leaned over and nudged her. "Come on. It won't be so bad."

Her lips thinned over her teeth in what she hoped at least partially resembled a smile of agreement.

She was going to kill Marie.

Justus rubbed his fingers over his upper lip and then stroked down around his chin. So he was going to have to dance with her. Well, that wouldn't be so bad. He just needed to keep his emotions in check. Remind himself that she only wanted to be friends. Keep things light. He could do that.

But judging by the look on Dakota's face, she'd rather kiss a toad than spend time dancing with him, which he had to admit rubbed him a little raw. Maybe he should just lay things out on the table? Tell her he was interested in getting to know her better for more than just friendship?

Before he could decide whether to say something to her right now, Marie stood and began directing traffic. "Darlene, thanks so much for making such a delicious brunch for us."

Darlene smiled and blushed, brushing away their applause and words of gratitude. "It was more than my pleasure. You all head on out to do the decorations, and as soon as I'm done here I'll be along to help with the final details and for the rehearsal."

"Great... so"—Marie glanced from Jalen to Riley— "Riley do you mind giving Jalen a ride to the church and stopping at the Wedding Shoppe on the way to pick up the candles and decorations? Then he can help you get all the candelabras and stuff into your back seat?"

Riley's fist clenched into a white-knuckled ball on the table.

Next to Justus, Dakota squirmed in her seat, a small frown puckering the yellow, bruised skin of her brow. Her blue eyes softened and filled with concern as she studied Riley, who remained quiet despite the fact that everyone was looking at her.

Jalen's jaw jutted off to one side, and Justus knew that memories of what had happened to his sister were probably at the forefront of his mind whenever he was around Riley.

He turned his attention back to Dakota. He knew she hadn't been doing this job very long. But it was obvious she cared for the woman across the table with every fiber of her being. How long had it been since he'd felt that way about any of his boys? He used to. Back in the beginning. Back when he had hope that he could make a difference. Now... He just wasn't sure anymore.

He darted a guilty look toward Jalen. Jalen would tell him he was an idiot to think he wasn't making a difference. But Jalen hadn't watched as Helene's body was zipped into a black bag. He hadn't stood by and seen the expressions on her parents' faces when the police had given them the bad news. He hadn't watched as Trey jumped the fence in his backyard just as a cop, with gun raised, yelled for him to stop...

Justus scrubbed a palm across his forehead and forced his thoughts back to the present.

Was there hope for a woman like Riley? Certainly not without the mercy of God.

Considering the cast on Riley's arm, her bruised eye, and the fact that she lived at House of Hope, it was obvious she'd suffered some sort of domestic abuse. If he remembered right, when he'd first met her last summer he'd had the impression she was expecting too. Based on all that, it was totally understandable that she'd be reluctant to ride alone in a car with a practical stranger – especially a man.

But... he frowned... She'd ridden with Jalen to House of Hope to get her things, and then to the church to help him look over the sound system. Justus darted a glance at Jalen. Had he said something to make her uncomfortable? He knew the man wouldn't have done anything to hurt her, but she certainly seemed a bit reluctant to go with him today.

Dakota leaned forward. "Maybe I should ride with Riley, and Jalen can ride with Justus?"

"No. It's okay." Riley shoved her hands into her lap, but not before Justus noticed they were trembling. "It will be fine." She tossed a tight little smile in Jalen's direction without actually meeting his gaze, then focused on a spot on the tablecloth in front of her.

Marie leaned forward to see Riley better. "As long as you're sure, Riley?"

Riley nodded. "Yes. I'm sure."

Dakota didn't say anything more, but there was a distinct sheen of moisture in her eyes that she quickly blinked away.

Justus eased back in his chair and folded his arms, swallowing hard. He hated seeing her hurt and yet loved her heart to help Riley all at the same time.

Dakota Trask was definitely a woman worth risking his heart for.

Decision made.

She might tell him to take his sentiment and go back home, but sometime today he would quit being a coward and just tell her he wanted to get to know her better.

Jalen rose a couple notches in Dakota's estimation when he held his silence and actually looked like he was happy they were making sure Riley was comfortable riding with him, instead of insulted that they might not trust him. She offered him a smile to let him know they weren't suspicious about him.

He gave her a nod of understanding and a subtle thumbs-up.

Marie glanced at a list lying in front of her. "Okay, good. So Justus and Dakota, if you don't mind, could you swing by Connie's Floral and pick up the swags and all the flowers? Reece and I are supposed to meet Pastor Mark for a few minutes this morning, and we also need to run by the bakery, because she wanted us to give the final okay on the cake before she delivers it tomorrow. Then we can all meet at the church at eleven thirty?"

Everyone agreed to their respective tasks, and Reece dismissed them all with, "Ready? And BREAK!"

Chapter 5

Riley pulled her car keys from her purse and subtly glanced at the guy who'd been saddled with babysitting her. Again.

A familiar roil of anger surged through her as she once again pondered how much she hated where she was in life right now. Nate had stolen so much from her. But not only from her. Also from those who were now putting themselves out to help her. From innocent guys like this one – what was his name again? – who suffered her insecurities without question and seemed fine with it. Why hadn't he gotten angry when they'd asked her that back there? Nate would have been beside himself if anyone had dared question whether she would be fine if she left with him – and strangely, no one had questioned her when she was with him, when in reality she'd have welcomed a lot of questioning. No one, that is, until Marie. Marie had questioned. Marie had made *her* question. And it was one of those questions that had raised Nate's anger to the point that he'd—

Pain shot across her palm and she realized she was squeezing the keys much too tightly. She eased her grip. Glanced again at the guy over the top of her car. How long had they been standing here with her staring into nothing?

He was waiting quietly, studying her with those seemingly all-seeing brown eyes of his. But not saying a word while she'd been spaced out for who knew how long.

Her brow slumped. "I'm sorry." She glanced down at the keys and then back to him. "Would you mind—" Her brain seemed incapable of creating full sentences.

But he'd apparently understood her because he appeared quietly at her side and reached out one hand, palm up, without touching her. "I'd be happy to drive."

She looked up into his eyes. And for some reason, the fear she'd expected to bloom instead wilted and slipped away. "I'm sorry about that back there." She gestured toward the house they'd just left. "My friends...they're just trying to take care of me. It's not about you."

His features softened. "I know. You're lucky to have friends like that who care about you so much."

She swallowed. Nodded. "Not everyone cares for others like that." Why had she said that? It revealed more than she was ready to. She gave her head a little shake to dispel the wave of dismay, and swung her attention to where Dakota was slipping into the passenger seat of a sporty red car while Justus held the door for her.

She could feel the guy studying her. But he remained very still. Like a nature lover afraid of scaring off a flighty animal.

As though he had some sort of magnetic force, her gaze returned to him. "I'm sorry. I know I've heard your name...?"

He smiled. "Well, now I am offended."

She blinked.

But his grin broadened and she realized he was teasing her.

She wished she could will herself to offer him a smile in return. He had a nice smile. A handsome broad face and teeth stark white against his brown skin. Kind chocolate-mocha colored eyes. Dark curly hair just mussed enough to give him a bit of a rakish look. A face so different from Nate's. Not just because Nate had been a red-head, but because Nate had never invited her scrutiny. He certainly wouldn't have stood so patiently for it.

Had Nate ever teased her? She chased the trail of history back to the very first time she'd met him and thought maybe he had back then. Back before... But all that had changed. She cradled her cast against her stomach and was surprised to feel her lips tip up at the corners, even if it was only just a bit.

He tilted his head, and his gaze skimmed her face. "It's good to see you at least try to smile. My name's Jalen Rivera." He stuck out one hand, but just held it there, letting her decide if she wanted to make the next move.

She took in his thick muscular palm. It was a shade lighter than the dark skin around it. Broad blunted fingers. A working man's calluses. Should she shake it? Why did every decision seem to take her forever lately? Just yesterday she'd stood for long minutes in the bread aisle, unable to make a decision on which loaf to buy.

This was silly. Why *wouldn't* she shake it? Finally she lifted her hand to his and her focus back to his face. "I'm Riley." That sounded dumb. Because she'd spent hours with him the other day. He probably thought she was the strangest woman he'd ever met. She probably *was* the strangest woman he'd ever met.

But he didn't belittle her. He only said, "Nice to meet you, Riley." His handshake was firm but gentle. Friendly. And then he released her and swept a gesture for her to move around the car since she'd asked him to drive. "I guess you know the way from here to the candle place, yeah?"

She nodded at him over the roof of her Kia and then slipped into the passenger seat. The smell of cigarette smoke had never been more appalling to her. Maybe because of the contrast between the memories the smell evoked, and her more recent experiences with these new friends. She tucked her thumbnail between her teeth, leaned her elbow against the car door and stared out across the rolling green lawn of Serenity Shores.

Jalen adjusted the seat and mirrors. Started the car. And then just sat there.

She turned to look at him.

He smiled gently. "At the end of the drive...which way do I turn?"

Of course. Directions. "Sorry. Right at the end of the drive."

"Right. Got it." His grin broadened. "You're a woman of few words, Riley. Am I going to turn right and just keep driving until I hit ocean somewhere when you disappear into your own world again?"

She studied him. The words could have been said with rancor. But there had only been gentle teasing and nothing else. A smile nudged for release for the second time that afternoon. "I'll try to stay present and remember to tell you where to turn."

He gave her a wink. "Alright then. Let's get those candles to the church, aye?"

Jalen hadn't said a word or even made a face or a noise about the smell of old cigarettes and spilled beer in her car.

And it really was quite nauseating. The smell of all the candles in the backseat was only going to make it worse.

She nibbled on her thumbnail without actually biting it. When she'd gotten pregnant she'd hoped that would make Nate quit smoking – in the car with her at least. But he had neither stopped smoking or drinking and—

A pain twinged through her arm, and she closed her eyes. Stay present. Stay focused. Now was not the time to revisit the nightmare that had been her life.

One day at a time she needed to walk into the future. She just wished it didn't look so bleak and gray.

"Take a right at the stop sign." She congratulated herself on the small victory and tried to relax into the seat. She could do this. Today was all she had to worry about now. Only today. Only herself. Only one more breath. Then another. And another after that.

And somehow, for the first time in her life, she'd found herself in the company of people who actually cared. They were kind. Loving.

There was that.

She pulled in another cool lungful of air. "Left here."

One day, one hour, one moment at a time. She could do this.

Dakota directed Justus to the florist's shop, and they loaded all the flowers carefully into his trunk so they wouldn't get smashed.

Justus had seemed a little nervous and jumpy all morning since Marie's announcement that they would have to dance together, and Dakota couldn't deny her own apprehension. Especially since he didn't know just how in jeopardy his toes were going to be yet.

He sank into the driver's seat and glanced over at her. He opened his mouth like he wanted to say something, but no sound emerged, and after a moment he snapped his jaw shut and thrust the keys into the ignition.

"Did you want to say something?"

He slapped one arm behind her seat and craned his neck to see behind them as he backed from their space. "It'll wait." He checked his side mirror, studiously avoiding her scrutiny.

She frowned. "Did I do something wrong?"

"No. Why would you say that?"

"Oh, I don't know. Maybe because when someone starts to tell you something and then stops it's usually because they don't know how to say it and that's usually because you've done something inappropriate."

"You haven't done anything wrong." He pulled onto the main road.

She waited for more, but he didn't even offer a hint at what he'd started to say. She propped her cast on the ledge of the door, and tamped down her irritation. Soon the main part of town was behind them and they were driving through the residential neighborhood near the church.

After several long silent minutes she let loose a sigh. "Justus, we do need to talk about your toes—" The last word emerged more like a screech as a dog, followed by a boy, darted across the road in front of them and Justus slammed on the brakes. Rubber screeched against pavement. She thrust her cast against the dashboard to keep from slamming into it.

The boy had stopped smack in the middle of the narrow road!

Her panic swelled. In less time than it took for one heart beat, the similarities to the night of her wreck back in high school slashed through her.

When the car skidded to a halt, they were only inches from the wide-eyed frozen stare of the freckle-faced boy. His dog was sitting obediently by the other side of the road, tongue lolling.

Justus loosed one short breath, and then he scrambled from the car. Judging by the look of anger chilling his eyes she wasn't sure what he had planned for the kid and scrabbled out her own door. "Justus!" She hopped on her one good leg toward them at the front of the car.

But Justus had only squatted down in front of the kid and gently turned him by the shoulders to face him. "Are you hurt?"

The kid shook his head, but he was trembling from head to toe.

Dakota begged her lungs to function and wiggled her fingers in her ears to chase away the shriek of brakes still resounding through the silence.

Justus jutted his jaw off to one side, but there was kindness in his expression as he studied the boy's face. "I could have killed you, kid. Do you live around here?"

"Yeah." The word was a bit flippant for someone

who'd just almost gotten run over.

"Well…" Justus flitted a glance toward the narrow space between the boy and his front bumper. "I think your guardian angel just got a whole lot skinnier."

A bubble of nervous laughter threatened to escape Dakota. She leaned one hand against the car and covered her mouth so the kid wouldn't think she was laughing at him. Her good leg trembled, nearly useless.

The boy only frowned. "What?"

Justus mussed his hair. "I just meant God was watching out for you. We just had a close call here. You know that, right?"

He nodded again.

The boy reminded her of someone. Who?

"Shouldn't you be in school?"

There was a beat before the kid said, "I'm homeschooled."

"I see. Well, I hope you've learned not to go dashing out into roads without a little double checking next time?" Sternness coated Justus's words.

"Sure. I guess."

Dakota closed her eyes. The scent of burnt rubber clung like smoke in the air. Nightmare images of the coastal highway not too far from here on a windy night peppered her mind. The sound of screeching tires and crunching metal could no longer be held at bay. The acrid odor stirred memories of the same smell mixed with blood and loamy earth.

She forced her eyes open and her attention onto Justus's broad shoulders where he still squatted in front of the child – a child who was healthy and whole and who would never understand how much pain and sorrow he could have caused for so many with his one careless moment of abandon.

"Good. Now..." Justus ruffled the boy's red hair gently. "Which side of this road do you live on?"

The boy pointed in the direction he and his dog had been running.

Justus scanned the empty road. "Alright then, go on. And please be more careful."

The boy ran off without another word.

Dakota met Justus's gaze and sank against the hood of the Z3 in relief.

Justus clasped his hands behind his head and paced several steps back and forth, his feet crunching against some gravel on the pavement, his cheeks puffed out in a combination of terror and thankfulness all in one. Finally he stopped and sank down onto the hood next to her. "That was way too close for comfort."

She nodded and eased a tremulous breath through pursed lips. "We should get out of the road. And I think the flowers are going to be a little worse for the wear." Her hands quaked as she reached to brush a strand of wind-whipped hair from her eyes and when she stood to hop around to her door, her good leg gave out from under her.

"Dakota!" Justus dove for her and managed to

break her fall, but not before they both ended up on the pavement.

And then she was crying. Great gulping sobs. And the memories that had been pushing for preeminence could no longer be staved off.

Justus's arms came around her, just like her arms had wrapped around Jason that night.

Chapter 6

Marinville, OR 2007

...After a year of living in Marinville while Daddy itinerated and raised money from churches to support their family for another four years on the mission field, the time had come for them to return to Africa. Dakota had been beside herself with tumultuous emotions that couldn't seem to decide where to settle. One moment she was thrilled to be returning to her friends at boarding school. The next moment she was grieving the loss of her friends in Marinville. One in particular. Jason Murton. Their flight, scheduled for the next day, took off at eight a.m. She wouldn't see Jason for a whole year until she graduated and came back to the States.

Jason rang the bell at their door that night. And when she opened it she could tell by the sheen in his eyes, he was feeling some of the same loss she was.

"Hi." She eased one shoulder onto the doorframe, leaving him on the stoop. He wore his leathers, his black Harley Davidson jacket broadening his shoulders. She worried the toe of her shoe through the fibers of their welcome mat, never taking her gaze off his face. "I'm glad you came."

He tilted his head and so much emotion caressed the one word he spoke. "Dakota..."

She reached out and took his hand, calling over her shoulder, "Mom, I'll be back in a couple hours, okay?" Without waiting for a reply she ran, pulling Jason after her down the walk.

He laughed. "Dakota, I'm here to help you pack remember? What are you doing?"

She stopped at his bike and sidled close to him, resting one hand on his chest. "Take me for a ride."

He shook his head. "I only have one helmet. And you don't have any protective gear."

"Jason." She tilted him a coy look and couldn't avoid the way her gaze dropped to his lips. "This will be our last night together for a whole year. Take me for a ride. It'll be okay. Just to Shady Shore. Just for a little bit. I'm almost done packing. We can finish when we get back."

He bent and pressed his forehead to hers. "As much as I want to we shouldn't. With only one helmet—"

Her lips separated the distance between them and settled on his. She felt his jolt of surprise that matched her own. Because while they'd come close to kissing a couple times, they'd never done so before. She pulled back, feeling the heat in her face. "Just to Shady Shore?" All she wanted was a few more intimate moments with him. Moments to cling to in the year ahead.

His gaze flitted to the road and back to her, and she knew he'd already relented. "Fine, but you have to wear the helmet. At least you're in jeans. My dad is going to kill me if he catches word of this."

She giggled. "I promise not to tell him."

Pain flickered over his features at the reminder she wouldn't be around for a long time to come. He settled the helmet over her head and adjusted the strap under her chin, then gave it a rap. "You good?"

She nodded.

"Alright. Let's do this." He swung a leg over his bike and waited for her to climb on.

She settled up close behind him and wrapped her arms around the warmth of his torso.

The motorbike roared to life, and he eased it out of the driveway.

Shady Shore was only a mile from her house. It should have been a short ride. Would have been if Jason hadn't been going over the speed limit and tossing a smile at her over his shoulder. Would have been except for the guy in the white pickup who'd been hurrying to the beach to go surfing after a few drinks at the bar. The guy who had swung a left in front of them as they came around the corner at the entrance just before Shady Shore.

One minute she and Jason were laughing with the wind in their faces and life stretching out long and full before them, and the next...nothing but searing anguish and darkness.

The doctors told Dakota the helmet saved her life.

The man in the truck walked away with a few scratches.

Jason hadn't been so lucky....

Justus swept Dakota up and strode to the side of the road. He settled her on her good leg and then wrapped his arms around her. Dakota shuddered and sniffled against his chest. Tightness constricted his breathing and his concern ramped up by the second. Had she been hurt? He didn't think so. As close as they had come to hitting the kid, the worst jolt would have been when he first hit the brakes.

Maybe almost hitting the kid was what had terrified her so badly?

He leaned sideways, trying to see her face, which was still buried against his chest. "Dakota? It's okay. We're all safe. The kid's safe. You're safe. I'm safe." He rubbed one hand over her back. "Everything's okay." The top of her head fit perfectly beneath his chin, and the vanilla and floral scent she always wore taunted him with its nearness. He swallowed and chastised himself for noticing how good she smelled when she was obviously only in need of a friend with a listening ear.

Another shudder coursed through her. "I'm sorry. I didn't mean to fall apart."

She said the words like she was pulling herself together, but she remained tucked in close to him, one hand fisted up near her mouth, her cast curled behind him.

His Z3 still idled in the middle of the road. He glanced down the street behind them and he was glad they were in a quiet residential neighborhood. No traffic being delayed because of them, so far.

"Your crying isn't about this incident, is it?"

It took a moment, but eventually she shook her head against his chest.

"Want to tell me about it?"

She sniffed. Remained quiet. And just when he was about to give up and suggest they get back in the car, she spoke. "I was in a wreck in high school. A friend died. It was my fault."

His eyes dropped closed and he held her a little tighter.

"We were on a m-motorbike. He only had one helmet, but I'd talked him into one last ride before I was supposed to leave for Africa the next day." The story tumbled from her, nightmarish detail after detail. Days in the hospital. How the man in the truck had walked away. How she'd learned about the death of her friend. Felt responsible.

He scooped one hand back through silky blonde strands and cupped her head gently as he rested one cheek against her hair. He couldn't help himself. He wanted to absorb all the pain she was feeling and take it on himself. "I'm sorry you went through something like that, so young."

Other than loosing a feathery sigh, she made no reply.

"The guy in the truck – was he drunk?"

"Not legally."

"Did he get convicted?"

She shook her head beneath his cheek. "His blood alcohol level was under legal. Jason was driving a few miles over the speed limit, and the guy in the truck was turning into the entrance to the park right as we came around the corner. They ruled it an accident."

"Who was the guy in the truck?"

She shook her head again. "I don't know. I was only awake for a short time at the scene before I fell unconscious and didn't revive till I was in the hospital. And no one ever mentioned to me who he was. We left for Africa two weeks later, right after Jason's funeral. I didn't ask. I've come really close to looking it up a few times. Or asking Jason's grandmother. But then I think... He must feel almost as terrible about the whole thing as I do, you know? Do I want to find out who he is? And then what? Would I go talk to him? Tell him I'm sorry that the accident was my fault? Or would I just not say anything to him but every sry time I saw him I'd remember... And what good would that do? I don't know. I've just decided up till now that it's better I don't know who it was."

"Jason's grandmother is in town?"

She dipped her chin. "Mrs. Murton."

"The lady from the hospital?"

"Yes. His parents moved away after... I'm not sure how long, but by the time I'd graduated and returned a year later, they had moved. But Mrs. Murton stayed. She's Jason's father's mother."

"Have you ever talked to her?"

Dakota shuddered. "Not about the accident. Someday I'll have to tell her it was my fault. But...I haven't gotten up the courage to do that yet."

Justus eased back from her and took her face in his hands. "Dakota, you were a kid. You made a mistake. But you can't live the rest of your life blaming yourself for Jason's death."

Big tears filled her eyes. "But it *was* my fault. He didn't want to go. Said he only had one helmet. That his father would be really angry if he found out he or his passenger had ridden without one. Then he insisted that I wear the helmet. So it is my fault."

He shook his head, willing her to believe him. "Did you force him to drive over the speed limit?"

She tucked one lip between her teeth. "No. But he was a daredevil. He always did that and I knew it."

The word "daredevil" hit him like a punch to the stomach and took him back to the first night he'd met Dakota and overheard her talking to herself. She'd called him an irresponsible daredevil. And that had been right after she'd reamed Reece out because she'd seen his motorbike in the drive and thought Reece had bought it.

He'd wondered at the time why she'd pegged him in such a negative light and with such hasty judgment. Now he understood.

Everything inside him went soft. She'd been carrying a big burden for a lot of years for one so young. "Neither did you make the guy in the truck turn at that exact moment. Nor did you place the entrance to that beach just around a corner. It was an accident."

She reached up and touched his face, sending a ping of awareness through him that he knew wasn't mutual. He forced himself to hold steady.

"Thank you for being such a caring friend." She smiled through her tears.

He suppressed a growl, knowing that she hadn't taken his admonishment to heart. A world of anguish still inhabited her expression. With his thumbs he gently swiped the tears from beneath her lashes, wishing he could infuse her with the truth and also wishing he had the right to kiss away her concerns.

He searched her face. Studied the tendrils of hair that caressed her still bruised and stitched temple. The dusting of tiny freckles scattered over her nose that were only visible because he was so close. Her full, slightly parted lips.

The emotions etching her face changed subtly, and her eyes widened a little. She bit her lip and eased back a step. "We should probably check on the flowers. I'm worried they might be a little banged up. And at the church they are probably wondering what's taking us so long."

He took a breath to dispel the lingering desire to kiss her, then slung her arm around his shoulders and helped her hop back to the car.

A quick check showed that the bouquets in the trunk had fared better than expected. All but the one which had apparently picked a fight with his tire iron and lost. The bouquet was smashed in one section.

Dakota gently pushed it back into its proper position and traced a finger over the damage. One of the roses had broken, and some of the foliage was crushed.

Justus gritted a grimace.

But Dakota seemed undaunted. "I can fix this, but let's get to the church first. I'll need scissors."

Chapter 7

The decorations were set. Jalen and Riley had put up all the candelabras. Dakota felt satisfied that she'd fixed the one smashed bouquet so nicely that not even she could tell which one had had the trunk mishap. And the church smelled fragrant and inviting.

They'd practiced the ceremony twice, and now Marie and Reece had gathered them together in the center of the church's reception hall. After all her crutching around and trips up and down the stairs throughout the day, Dakota's good leg was about done for and her arm was aching intensely. But she was doing this for Marie, and she didn't want to disappoint her. So she leaned heavily against her crutches and hoped no one would notice her discomfort.

It was only a moment before Justus strode up with a chair and plunked it beside her. "Sit down before you fall down," he said quietly.

She wrinkled her nose at him, but did as he'd

commanded. Her leg trembled as she lowered herself into the chair. She still couldn't believe she'd fallen apart like that in front of him. She quite honestly hadn't broken down over the situation for years. And now, just when she'd like to find a nice dark hole to crawl into so she didn't have to endure any more of his scrutiny, she had to learn to dance with him. And on one leg that was barely working and another that was strapped into a boot the size of Rhode Island.

Marie was so excited over the dance, she didn't seem to notice Dakota's predicament. Marie rubbed her hands together, and a gleam frolicked in her gaze as she scanned the group. Alyssa skipped over and climbed up onto Dakota's lap. Despite the fact that she only wanted to have a few minutes to massage her leg, Dakota snuggled her close and managed to only grimace once when the little girl's bony hip ground into her cramping thigh.

Justus squatted by the chair. "Hey Alyssa, how would you like to sit on my shoulders for a bit?"

"Yes!" The little girl scrambled from Dakota's lap so fast one might have thought he'd offered her a lifetime supply of candy.

Dakota gave Justus a look of thanks. He only nodded and squatted down so Alyssa could scrabble up his back and onto his shoulders.

Good with kids. Chalk up another tally mark in the pros column. Not that she was keeping track.

"Okay you guys," Marie called for their attention. "I saw the looks you all were giving us this morning, and I know this is asking a lot from all of you, but I promise you we are going to have fun with this. So here's how it's going to go. First our song, 'I Will Always Love You', is going to start out nice and slow and Reece and I are going to start the dance, then the song is going to splice into a faster version and we want you six to come in. We're going to do a little routine that will be fun and wow all the guests, and then it will morph back to the slow version and will end with just Reece and me on the floor again."

"What about me, Mommy?" Alyssa called from her perch. "Do I get to dance?"

Marie smiled at her. "Not this first dance, baby. You will get a chance to dance with Reece later, but for this one you're going to sit with Grandma, okay?"

Alyssa bent around and peered into Justus's face, her eyes all asparkle. "Mr. Reece is going to be my daddy!"

Justus gave her a smile. "And I bet he's going to be a good one, too, don't you think?"

"Yep." Alyssa gave a definitive nod of her little head. "Yep, I do."

Reece's feet shuffled, and he kicked at something on the floor with the toe of his cowboy boot.

Dakota felt the sting of the tears that sprang into her eyes. She had loved watching God bringing this family together, and now tomorrow their long journey would finally come to both an end and a beginning.

Something made her glance up at Justus. Justus frowned, taking in her tears. He glanced from her to Reece and back again, a look of speculation in his gaze. And with dread Dakota realized he'd mistaken the reason for her emotional state.

But it was too late to quietly correct him, because Marie was dispersing them to the spots she wanted them to enter the dance floor from, and Justus was busy setting Alyssa down and pointing her in the direction of her grandmother.

When they once again stood side by side, he was stiff and sullen.

"Justus," she whispered his name, wetting her lips as she waited for his attention, because somehow it was suddenly very important to her that he understand she did not have feelings for Reece.

He dropped his focus to her.

She shook her head. "My tears were ones of happiness for what God is doing in the lives of my friends, and not for any other reason."

His brow lowered. "So...you don't have feelings for him?"

She shook her head. "No. But I do have a confession to make..."

He folded his arms and leaned into his heels. "A confession?"

"I can't dance."

Brows arched, he gave her a bit of an exasperated look. Then he chuckled. "You're serious?"

She grinned. "Utterly and completely. I've never danced a day in my life, and I'm going to have to learn with a gimpy leg. You and I are probably going to end up in a heap on the floor."

His laugh was full and long this time. "That's what you started to tell me back in the car before the boy ran out in front of us, wasn't it? You said we needed to talk about my toes and—" he scratched his head— "I have to tell you, I had this whole image of you wanting me to take my shoes off so you could look at my feet. I was a little worried, and my weird-girl-radar was clanging pretty loudly."

Reece and Marie's song started, and Dakota leaned a little closer to him to be heard over the notes. "You want weird-girl? You're about to experience her firsthand"

He grinned. "You are stressing about this just a little too much. You just go out there and move your feet in time to the music. We don't have to look all professional, or anything. Just follow my lead. It's a basic four-step song."

She gave him a pointed look and thrust her booted foot into the air.

He chuckled this time. "My dad used to have my sister stand on his feet. We could have you do that to me."

A blush washed over her at the mere thought of being so close to him, not to mention smashing his toes with her weight. "I think I'll take my chances, thanks."

"Okay, so we have a few seconds before our part. Let me show you."

Before she could even blink, he stepped right in front of her and took her crutches. He leaned them against a table to their right, then rested his hands on her shoulders and studied her carefully. "How's your ankle? You going to be able to do this?"

The way his nearness was impacting her, if she fell flat on her face it would have nothing to do with her twisted ankle, she felt sure about that. She managed a nod and wished she could pull up even one of the items on her cons list.

"So..." he cleared his throat. "This hand goes here." He lifted her right hand to his left shoulder and settled one palm against her waist, clasping her other hand with his free one. "And the steps are easy. I start with my left leg and you with your right. You are going to step back while I step forward."

"Backward!?" She tossed a glance behind herself to make sure the path was clear.

He gave her a trust-me look. "Don't worry. I won't run you into anything, I promise. Ready? So two steps back..." He guided her through the moves and she felt like a stiff marionette on broken strings. He was chuckling by the time they finished the second step. "And then one step to your right like...so." He squeezed her hand gently. "Good. And then we repeat." The music's pace picked up. "And this is our cue to step in, so here we go." He spun her out onto the floor, and Dakota spent the whole first round counting steps and making sure her feet followed Justus's lead.

The music wound down and Marie clapped her hands in delight. "Thanks you guys! This is going to be so special and mean so much to us." She motioned to the person in the sound booth to cue the music up again. "Let's go through it one more time just so you're all comfortable with the steps, and then we'll work on positioning and putting it all together." Both Reece and Kylen groaned audibly, and both Marie and Taysia smacked them at the same moment. Dakota snickered as Marie called, "Not much longer, I promise" and the music started.

If she'd thought being so near to Justus the first time around had been bad, this time was infinitely worse. Mostly because she was comfortable enough now with the easy rhythm that she didn't need to stare down at their feet or count her steps, and she wasn't quite sure where to look.

She concentrated on the center of his T-shirt but then became aware of the ripple and play of well-defined muscle beneath the dark blue cotton and liked it just a little too much. Her face heated and she tossed him a quick glance to see what he was doing.

His attention was fixed on her face, his lips tipped up in bemusement. "You're a fast learner, Dakota Trask." He leaned slightly closer. "And very pretty when you blush." One eyelid dropped in a quick wink.

She wanted to look away. Should look away. But her eyes refused the instructions her brain tried to send them. Feeling the pulse of heat beating in time with her heart, she tucked her lower lip between her teeth. "That's a little bold for 'just friends', don't you think?" Her outright flirtation surprised her and increased the temperature of her face even more. She did manage to look away then. But only for a second and then she was once again entrapped by the blue magnetism of his gaze.

His voice was warm and low. "Mmmmm, maybe." The humor in his expression seeped away, and his focus drifted from her eyes to her hair, brushed across both her cheeks, and swept down to her lips, where it paused. He swallowed and seemed to give himself a little shake. And then the intensity in his gaze was gone, replaced again with his casual soft scrutiny.

The song ended and he released her. She gimped a couple steps away to give herself some space and get a hold of her emotions.

Marie floated over, all aglow, and wrapped Dakota in a big hug. "Thanks for all you've done to help me prepare for tomorrow. I couldn't have done this without you!"

Happy for the distraction, Dakota hugged her back. "Absolutely. I'm so thrilled for you guys."

"Are you thrilled for me, Aunt Kota?"

Dakota bent to peer into the round face with sincere brown eyes and bopped Alyssa on the nose. "Yes. I'm thrilled for you too."

They spent the next thirty minutes practicing a bit of choreography for the dance, and Dakota prided herself on the fact that she was somehow able to morph into work mode and simply get the learning done without thinking about the man she was dancing with...too much.

Finally Marie called, "Alright everyone, our reservations at the restaurant are in thirty minutes, so let's all mosey on that way, okay?"

Dakota's stomach rumbled, reminding her she hadn't eaten since breakfast earlier that morning. Justus hadn't either. He was probably practically famished if he was anything like her brother.

Justus appeared at her side with her crutches and held them out to her.

Alyssa tilted her head and gave Dakota a serious assessment as she tucked the crutches under her arms. "Aunt Kota looks tired. You should give her a piggybackride so she doesn't have to hop up all those stairs."

Dakota's eyes shot wide and she spun to look at Justus. "Uh..."

Justus was no help. He only folded his arms and raised his eyebrows at her, a bit of a devilish grin tipping his lips.

She spun back to Alyssa. "I'm fine, honey. Thanks for thinking of me. But I'm too big for Mr. Justus to give a piggyback ride to."

Alyssa shrugged in a "whatever" gesture and followed her mother toward the stairs.

Justus leaned close, one hand settling at the

small of Dakota's back as he spoke low in her ear. "I can think of worse things than having your arms around me." The warmth of his breath brushed her cheek.

A trickle of pure bliss tripped down her spine and spread through her extremities in a warm wave. But she slammed her teeth together refusing to give the feeling roots. The problem was she didn't *want* to feel warmth spreading through her extremities. She'd much rather that she was repulsed by his attention. But somehow he was breaching all her carefully constructed barriers. Why couldn't she be attracted to some guy who wore pocket protectors for a living? One who would go to a nice safe work environment every day and come home to her and the kids every night? But no! She had to be attracted to an ex-con who worked with kids who were a danger to society for his living. He was just as likely to get shot on the job as to come home at night. After losing Jason, she didn't know if she could go through something like that again.

She gave him as scathing a look as she could muster, which, because of a traitorous smile that slipped free, she feared came out more like a coy invitation than a "back off" warning.

A twinkle lit his gaze. And his warm laughter filled all the nooks and crannies of her heart as he stretched out one hand for her to precede him.

Chapter 8

Justus fisted the lining of his pockets as he ushered Dakota into the restaurant. He hadn't found the words yet to tell her he wanted more than friendship. But maybe that was a good thing. If he did end up going back to Deschutes Rejuvenation could he ask her to come with him? Then again...what were the chances he was going back? He sighed.

The room Reece and Marie had reserved at Fisherman's Wharf for their reception dinner was an intimately curtained alcove in one corner of the dining area. Glass walls on two sides of the table faced the beach and ocean, but since sheer white curtains had been pulled to block the brightness of the low-hanging sun outside, it was mostly the soft warm red drapes and candlelight that caught Justus's attention. That and the chin-height blonde woman leaning on her crutches at his side.

He took a second to study her, since her attention was fixed elsewhere at the moment.

Today she wore her long blonde hair straight and flowing past her shoulders. Her oval face glowed with happiness as she watched Reece seat Marie at the head of the table. Her lips turned up just slightly, and joy crinkled the corners of her lake-blue eyes.

He swallowed. Definitely a face a guy would love to wake up to for the rest of his life. But he had no right to be staring, as evidenced by her wrinkled nose that suddenly captured his focus. She'd caught his scrutiny.

He purposely held her gaze, lifted his brows, and dropped her a wink. He did it because the pink that touched her cheeks had enchanted him often this afternoon and he wanted to see it one more time. He wasn't disappointed for his efforts.

She looked down and leaned more heavily on her crutches.

He wasn't acting like much of a gentleman. Quickly he remedied that by pulling out the nearest chair for her. She'd been a real trooper this afternoon but he knew her ankle and arm were probably throbbing to beat the band right about now.

"Thanks." She sank into her seat.

He took the crutches from her and walked them to the corner and leaned them there before returning to take his seat next to her. "How are you doing? Do you need any pain killers?"

Weariness seemed to drape her features. "Actually, I think I will take something. I've got a pretty bad headache coming on."

He watched her fumble through her purse and felt a wave of concern. She'd probably been on her feet far too long today. And he knew she'd stayed up much too late last night doing all the calligraphy on the tent cards for the tables at the reception. She had the bottle of pills in her hand now, but her hands were trembling, and she seemed to be having a hard time with the cap. "Here, let me." He took the bottle and opened it, then handed it back to her. "Do you want me just to take you back to Serenity Shores? You've been on your feet a long time today."

"No. No." She shook her head and gave him a smile he felt sure was forced. "I'll be fine in a few minutes. Just had a wave of exhaustion wash over me a minute ago. But I think it's simply from being in a bit of pain all day long." She swallowed down two of the pills.

"Marie's lucky to have a friend like you." He meant it. Dakota was a person who would always put the needs of another above her own.

Dakota grinned at him. "She'd be luckier if I could dance."

He chuckled. "You did just fine."

"Thanks to you."

He shrugged and lifted his hands. "What can I say? We're good together."

Her lips thinned like she thought he probably expected her to smile at that but her heart wasn't really in it.

Back off, Justus. Give her some space.

The problem was, the more time he spent with her, the less he wanted to give her space.

Riley couldn't believe she'd missed the fact that the rehearsal dinner was going to be held at Fisherman's Wharf. It took nearly every morsel of resolve she possessed to climb from the car in the parking lot when Jalen pulled into a spot in front of the log and stone building. Golden light spilled from the large windows, and the setting sun had washed the sky behind the building a pale pink, but the ambiance did nothing to sooth the rapid beating of her heart. Nor did it make the suddenly illusive oxygen any more prevalent.

If not for Jalen's steady assessment, she might have just given in to the desire to curl herself into a little ball and rock the past several years away. But he was there. And his seemingly all-seeing gaze was fastened to her as though he sensed something was wrong even though she felt certain she'd given no visible reaction. So she drew in a calming breath and forced one foot in front of the other.

Through dinner and all the chit chat she held her silence, picking at her food and doing her best to look like she was having a good time. Thankfully Marie was so enthralled and excited, she wasn't her normally observant self, and everyone else was keeping her busy.

But now, dinner was over and Riley'd really had about all that she could take of the room. Maybe God was tormenting her because, even though the tables were arranged slightly differently, the place she wound up sitting was almost the exact location where she'd sat as she waited for Nate to arrive for their date that night all those years ago. The night her life had started to fall utterly and completely apart. Before that summer night, at least she'd had some tattered rags to grab onto – and she'd been clinging to them for all she was worth, even though doing so was threatening to pull her limb from limb. She'd even tried to get Nate to marry her.

But after that night. After the wreck. And the boy who'd been killed...Nate had just never been the same.

She remembered the feel of her phone vibrating. Thinking Nate must have gotten tied up at work. Glancing down. Seeing that it was the hospital calling. She remembered the wave of dread that had washed over her. How a seagull had swept past the window and cavorted with a breeze as she'd pressed her phone to her ear and answered with a tremulous, "Hello?"

Her hands clenched so hard they trembled.

Beside her Jalen shifted. "Everything okay?"

She'd have liked to tell him to take his quiet attentiveness and eat it. But the last thing she wanted was to make Marie feel bad for having her rehearsal dinner here. It wasn't her fault, after all, that Nate had chosen to go drinking and surfing after work that day instead of coming straight here like they'd planned. Not her fault a kid had died. Not her fault that Nate had let his guilt eat away the rest of his humanity.

Jalen was still watching her.

She waved away his concern. "I just need a bit of air." She stood and headed for the nearest door, which took her out onto the restaurant's back deck.

Dinner must have taken even longer than she'd thought because moonlight now glinted off the undulating surface of the inky ocean. The soft *shush*ing of the waves did nothing to sooth her like it normally did. Her cast clunked against the rail as she rested her forearms on it, and suddenly she couldn't hold the tears at bay for another moment. What was she supposed to do with her life? She couldn't live at House of Hope expecting others to take care of her forever, especially now that the house needed to be rebuilt and she was just an extra burden to everyone.

And to add insult to injury, she missed Nate. She must be losing her mind. Nate had stolen *everything* from her, even her child – *their* child – and she could only think how she wished she could see his face just one more time.

Anger at her continued weakness surged through her. Consign the man to the vilest region of hell, if hell even existed, which she doubted. If there was a God, He'd certainly given her the short end of the stick when it came to blessings. And since everyone always talked about God's love, she had to conclude He didn't exist. How loving was it for Him to put her in a home with a workaholic for a father? A mother who had to be at every social event, charity auction, or country club shindig that offered alcohol, and who was always emotionally barricaded behind the Great Wall of China? What kind of God would let an accident like that happen and allow Nate to become so cruel without consequences? No...if God was love, nothing in her life showed proof of His existence. And yet...there were good, kind, loving people like Marie and Dakota who believed in Him...

Behind her, the door opened, and soft footsteps crossed the deck.

She balled up her fists and dashed at the moisture on her cheeks with her wrists. Why couldn't he just leave her alone?

Jalen stopped beside her and held out her coat. "Figured you'd be getting cold out here."

He was right, but she hadn't noticed until he mentioned it. She accepted the jacket and jerked it around her shoulders. "Thanks."

He folded his broad hands together, leaned against the rail and studied the star sprinkled sky above them.

She wished he would go inside and leave her alone to enjoy her misery.

She heard him swallow, and then he spoke so softly she almost didn't hear the words. "My sister's husband killed her."

A jolt of shock spun her towards him.

His gaze remained fixed on the night sky. "I was sixteen when it happened. We all knew he didn't treat her right. But none of us thought it would go that far or even close, I guess. One night he just...lost it... He's serving life down in Salem now." He turned his back to the rail and rested his elbows on it, looking her right in the face. "She's one of the reasons I work with Justus at Deschutes Rejuvenation. I figure if I can reach one or two of those boys before they become like my brother-in-law, I'll be doing my part for this world. What God put me here for." He tilted his head, his eyes soft and full of understanding. "He'll help you find your place too, Riley. But you have to give yourself time."

She smirked. She couldn't help herself. "You think God has a plan for me, Jalen?"

His brows went up. "You don't?"

A bark of cynical laughter popped free before she could prevent it. She held up her cast and then gestured to the eye she knew was still red and ugly. "Maybe God's plans are for me to be some man's punching bag?"

A muscle ticked in Jalen's jaw, and a sheen of moisture filled his eyes. But he held his silence, only studying her with something like disappointment in his expression.

And she hated that she'd hurt him. Sure she'd been going to church with Marie and Dakota for weeks, but that didn't mean she was buying into all the rhetoric. She spun away from him before she did something really stupid like collapse into his arms. "Go away, Jalen. I just need some time to myself."

The deck creaked, and she felt the barest caress of his fingers against her shoulder. "I'm praying for you, Riley." And then he slipped quietly back into the restaurant.

Dakota felt a wave of concern as Jalen came into the room. He looked troubled. She stood and strode toward him, doing her best to ignore the pain pulsing through her foot. "Jalen?"

He rested his hands on his hips and pressed his lips together, shaking his head. "Something isn't right, Dakota. Something about this place has her even more on edge than usual. I'm worried about her."

She touched his arm. "I'll go talk to her."

The chill breeze seemed to bite into every pore as Dakota stepped out onto the deck. She tucked her arms together and stopped at the rail next to Riley.

Riley glanced over, but from the look on her face it was obvious she didn't want to talk to anyone. Her jaw jutted off to one side and she snorted. "He send you out here to make sure I wasn't going to jump off into the water?" Immediately Riley's face cringed. "I'm sorry. I shouldn't have said that." She waved a hand, encompassing the beach, the ocean, the restaurant behind them. "I'm just...in a mood I guess."

Dakota hunched into her shoulders and leaned

on the rail beside her. "Want to talk about it?"

Riley sighed. She rubbed the back of her neck, staring down into the dark shadows on the sand below them. "Not sure there's much to talk about that I haven't already rehearsed half to death." She pointed back into the restaurant. "This is the place where Nate's and my life started to fall apart. Well, actually Nate started to pull it apart before that night but... I was here waiting for him... We were supposed to have dinner. He was late. I thought he'd just gotten tied up at work. But..." She laughed bitterly. "Turned out that Nate was more interested in drinking and surfing than in having dinner with me."

Dakota frowned, not sure she was quite following the disjointed story but a strange buzzing—a begging for attention—danced at the edges of her mind.

Riley seemed to be on a roll, and if Dakota's face had paled at all she didn't seem to notice. Her finger jabbed back toward the restaurant once more. "I was sitting at a table pretty close to where we were tonight, waiting for him to come. My phone rang. It was the hospital. Nate had been in a wreck out on 101. A kid was killed. Just a young guy not even out of high school yet. He was riding his motorbike with his girlfriend."

Dakota felt the strength leaving her knees. The rail took most of her weight, and it was only by sheer will that she kept on breathing.

Riley's voice trembled when she continued.

"Nate was never the same after that. He'd been a little hard around the edges before then, but after that... He just... Well... That's when our lives took the turn that brought us to this." She gestured to her cast and blood-red eye.

Dakota clung to the rail for dear life, the headache that had been plaguing her all evening sprung to the fore with new vengeance. Her jaw dropped open but she couldn't seem to find even one word to say. She was supposed to be comforting and counseling Riley. She needed to get a grip.

"The crazy thing is," Riley continued, "I was sitting in there just now feeling all miserable and of all the crazy things missing Nate. *Missing* him!" She cursed. "After all he did to me... You'd think I would be relieved now that he's gone." She scooped a hand back through her hair. Suddenly Riley stilled and Dakota realized she was looking at her. A frown pinched Riley's brow. "Did I say something wrong?"

Dakota became aware that both her hands were covering her mouth. She lowered them slowly and shook her head, but she could do nothing to stop the tears that were flowing down her cheeks. "No, no... I just... That was the summer of 2007, right?"

Riley nodded, a puzzled frown bunching her brow.

Dakota fumbled for the right words. "I was the girl. The girlfriend."

And then the sudden understanding of all she truly was responsible for washed through her. "Oh

Riley, oh Riley." She groped for something to sit down on. The deck, and the restaurant and the ocean were all spinning around her in a dizzying vortex, but there was nowhere to sit. She buried her face against her forearms and sobbed for all the pain a single bad choice had leveled on the world.

"Dakota? I'll get help." Riley's footsteps slapped across the boards, and the door to the restaurant *whoosh*ed open.

Somewhere at the back of her mind she realized if she didn't pull herself together Marie's reception dinner would be ruined, but Dakota couldn't find the strength to stop Riley. *Dear God. Dear God. Dear God!* She thought of Riley's baby, a little boy who had been denied his first breath at the hands of his angry father....

...And the chain of events that led to that moment shot straight as an arrow back through time and landed directly on her doorstep.

Chapter 9

Justus watched quietly as Jalen stepped back inside from the deck and said a few words to Dakota. He scrubbed the back of his neck with one hand and twisted his empty, upside down coffee cup around on its saucer with the other.

All evening he had been pushing away the niggling reminder that tomorrow was the wedding and after that he had to make a decision about what to do with the rest of his life. He'd given eight years trying to reach boys who were heading down a path that could lead only to trouble. Up until a few weeks ago, if anyone had asked him if he felt like his job made a difference he would have unequivocally replied that of course it did. Troubled boys came to his program, and responsible young men exited it.

That's what he *would* have said...

But Treyvon McAllister had changed all that.

Justus massaged the skin between his eyes, and battened down the curl of nausea in his gut.

Treyvon McAllister had come to him much like any of his other boys came to him. Much like he himself had been before he ended up in the system. Trey's grades had dropped at school. He'd ended up in juvy a couple times, always angry at home, never respectful to anyone in authority...

The principal had called Justus. Asked if he had any room. Enrollment had already been at its peak, but Justus had made space on the roster for one more kid. He converted the storage closet at the end of the dorm into another bedroom. And he'd poured his heart and soul into Treyvon McAllister.

He'd even thought he was reaching the troubled boy. Trey had quit complaining about morning devotions, he'd started doing his list of chores without constant reminders, and he had also started pitching in to help a couple other kids with their chore list from time to time. His grades had improved along with his attitude. So when graduation day rolled around, Justus hadn't even hesitated to give him a passing grade and send him home.

Trey hadn't been home for even a week when Justus had been awakened in the middle of the night by frantic pounding on his door. Half asleep and still rubbing his eyes, he'd stumbled down to his entry and fumbled with the lock to find Trey's mother covered in blood, sobbing and trembling on his front stoop.

"You havta come, Mista Teague! You havta come! My Trey he didn't mean it. I swear to you he never meant it."

A cold wash of horror swept through Justus as he took her in from head to toe. "Are you hurt Mrs. McAllister?"

"No, no. Not me. You havta come! Come now, Mr. Teague." She'd grabbed his arm and tugged.

Justus came back to the present when Jalen sank into the chair beside him.

He was trembling, he realized. He clasped his hands together and shoved them under the table, then tipped a nod toward the deck. "Everything okay?"

Jalen stretched his feet out in front of him and leaned into the slats of his chair, folding his arms. "Not sure, to be honest. Something's been bothering Riley ever since we pulled into the parking lot out front. She's quiet normally, but tonight... Well, something more was going on. Dakota is out there talking to her now."

The waitress came by and set generous slices of cherry cheesecake before them. "Would you gentlemen care for a cup of coffee?" she asked.

Justus turned his cup over and nodded his acquiescence. "Thanks." He forked off a bite of the cheesecake and chewed without really tasting as Jalen did the same.

His thoughts returned to the past.

As Mrs. McAllister had run to her old Nissan still idling in the drive, he'd hastily dialed Jalen to let him know what was going on. Thankfully they were between terms and had no other boys on campus. He grabbed a jacket, and followed Mrs. McAllister back to her house all the while trying to assure himself that if it were a real emergency she would've called 911. But her hysteria bothered him. That and the fact that before they left his place he hadn't been able to get any more information out of her.

Jalen cleared his throat. "Mind handing me the cream?"

Justus worked his jaw from side to side to keep the words of frustration bottled up inside. Jalen didn't take cream in his coffee, and well he knew it. He picked up his coffee cup only to find his hand trembling again, and set it back down.

Jalen eyed him speculatively. "You ready to talk about it?"

Justus shoved his dessert and coffee away from the edge of the table and rested his face in his palms. "Not now, Jalen. There will be time enough for reality after the wedding. I don't want to ruin this day for Reece and Marie."

Jalen snorted. "The truth is you've helped more boys over the years than you could count if you wracked your brain for a month, and you're letting one boy's poor choices make you question all the good you've done over the past eight years. They were terrible choices – horrendous choices – yes. But they were his choices, not yours."

The familiar spout of horror and frustration that had been riding close to the surface lately threatened to erupt in a geyser of anger. But he clenched his teeth and managed to hold his silence.

Mrs. McAllister had turned the corner onto their street, her taillights jittering in a shorted-out flicker that felt oddly appropriate for the circumstances.

Justus had thought through the gamut of possibilities, and by the time he pulled into the McAllister's garbage-littered driveway, he'd convinced himself that since Mrs. McAllister had driven all the way to his place to get him nothing could be too terribly wrong.

He clambered from his car at the end of the drive. It was a cold miserable night. Pacific Northwest rain hung in a thick cloud of mist, the kind that soaked through even the hardiest of rain jackets and clung to skin with damp clammy claws.

He huddled into his collar and felt relieved to see that Mrs. McAllister seemed calmer as she waited for him in the weak beam of the streetlight at the end of the walk. Treyvon had an old girlfriend who'd brought nothing but trouble into his life. Justus fully expected to find that Treyvon had fallen back in with the wrong crowd, done something stupid, and gotten himself beat up for it.

So when Mrs. McAllister led him through the kitchen's back door and he saw Helene lying in a congealing puddle of blood on the chipped yellowed tiles, shock threw his hands to his head.

Trey sat huddled in one corner of the kitchen, his arms wrapped around his ears. A black hole with crumbling edges marred the plaster above his head. He was rocking back and forth like a little boy who needed soothing and didn't even look up when they entered.

Justus's hand trembled as he reached for his phone. He knew by the staring eyes before he even bent and touched the pulse point in her throat that Helene was dead. But the stillness beneath her cold skin confirmed it.

Treyvon finally glanced up with wide, wild eyes. "I didn't mean it, Mr. Teague. I didn't mean to hit her so hard."

Justus had no words. He swallowed down bile as he tapped in 911 with a shaky finger.

Mrs. McAllister turned from where she'd set her purse on the cluttered counter. Her gaze fastened on the phone in his hand. "No!" She lurched at him, almost knocking the phone free. "You can't turn him in! You can't turn in my boy!" She clawed at his arm. "I done got you so's you'd help him! My Trey didn't mean it! He didn't!"

"This is 911, what is your emergency?"

Justus held up one arm to fend off the crazed mother who was still punching and clawing and hitting.

"I-I need to report a...death," he called over the commotion.

"Sir, can you tell me your address?" Rapid-fire typing sounded in the background.

Justus felt like every thought had to be pulled from a miry bog. Mrs. McAllister was kicking him now and scratching at him as he held her at arm's length from the phone. "Uh, give me a minute..." He tried to grab Mrs. McAllister's hands without success, and grunted when one of her fists connected with his ribs. "Mrs. McAllister, stop! What's your house number?"

The woman only screeched and clawed. "Gimme that phone! You can't turn in my boy. He done turned eighteen. This will be the end of him!"

On the other end of the line the dispatcher spoke in his ear, "Sir, are you safe?"

Mrs. McAllister might be violent, but she was less than half his weight and only as tall as his chest. "Stop, Mrs. McAllister. Just stop." He finally grabbed a handful of her sweatshirt and held her against the kitchen cabinets.

"Mama..." Trey continued to rock. "What have I done, Mama?"

Like a cloak of civility had been dropped over her, Mrs. McAllister pulled away and darted to her son's side. She clutched his head to her bosom. "Oh my baby. My poor, poor baby." She rubbed his back as though maybe he'd been the one who was injured.

Angling away from her, Justus spoke to the woman on the other end of the line once more. "Please send some units."

"Sir, I need you to confirm your exact location for me."

Justus stepped out onto the deck and searched the front of the house for a house number, but there was none. "Listen, my name is Justus Teague. I run Deschutes Rejuvenation out on Highway 97. I'm at the home of one of my former students. I followed his mother here. There's no house number on the front of the house and I don't remember it. We're on Seventh in Terrebonne. If you come in from Central, it's the last house on the northwest side of the street, and there is an old rusty pickup in the front yard."

It had only taken the police a few minutes to arrive. The coroner had pronounced Helene dead a few minutes later and Justus had stood by while she was placed into the county hearse. A movement in his peripheral vision caught his attention. Trey was sprinting across the yard in a hard line for the fence. "Trey stop!"

The officer next to him was only a millisecond behind in reaction. "Freeze right there!"

Trey kept going. He leapt up, his hands scrabbling for the top of the fence.

A single shot rang out.

Mrs. McAllister screamed.

Trey collapsed onto the grass.

And Justus was sprinting towards him before he even realized he was moving.

Blood gushed from a jagged hole in Trey's pants, soaking his leg and the grass below him. "They done shot me!" he groaned.

And then Justus was being dragged back. One

officer stood over the boy with a gun, while another officer yanked his arms behind him and cuffed him.

Trey screamed and writhed.

Justus felt the damp soaking into his knees. The cold air stung his lungs. He would never forget the surreal feeling that had overwhelmed him as the flashing lights of the vehicles reflected off the mist around him. How his breath had fogged the air as an EMT had quickly set to work on Trey's leg to stop the bleeding. How Mrs. McAllister's screams tore through the night over and over and over again.

Trey had begged him to ride with him to the hospital, and Justus had agreed, though now he could only remember the ride and the following night in snatches. He'd gone with the police at some point to Helene's parents' home. Stood by quietly wishing he could offer something, anything, of comfort as the news tore them in two. But he'd had nothing. Nothing other than his own grief and the feeling that he should have been able to do something to prevent this.

With Trey's confession of guilt, his case had moved through the courts fairly quickly. Just last week the decision had come down. Trey had gotten twenty-five years with the possibility of parole after fifteen. He would be thirty-three.

Justus now had to find the courage, the forgiveness—the ability to extend hope and not extinguish it—to go see the kid.

If he were anything like Mick, he would have

already done so. He rubbed the place below his collarbone where his one and only tattoo resided and released a short breath. Unlike Mick, Jesus still had a long way to go in transforming Justus's heart into one like His.

Justus could feel Jalen still pointedly glowering at him.

Justus sighed. "I know, Jalen. I know. How many years have you known me? I've never been one to give up easy, but this...took the wind out of my sails, I guess. I know D.R. does a lot of good for boys. I'm just not...I need to be sure that's where I'm still supposed to be." At the thought of giving up the ministry he'd served for the past eight years something roiled in the pit of his stomach. "I still feel like I want to help boys. I'm working on it. I just need some ti—"

The door from the back deck suddenly slammed open bringing Justus to a halt.

Riley's eyes were wide and frightened and fixed directly on him. "Something's wrong with Dakota."

A jolt of alarm so powerful it almost took the strength from his legs shot through him. He bolted up and dashed past Riley.

But by the time he got outside, Dakota was striding across the deck from near the rail. She held up a hand. "I'm fine. Let's not ruin Marie and Reece's dinner, but can you just take me home, please?"

His concern lowered several notches, but he

scanned her from head to toe just to make certain she looked alright. "Riley said something was wrong?" Behind him he heard the door open again and Riley stepped around him, concern still etching her features.

Dakota turned and pulled a startled Riley into an embrace. "I'm sorry. So sorry. I didn't mean to fall apart. It's just...we need to talk. But right now, I need to think some things through. And we've got the wedding tomorrow. So...give me a few days, okay?"

Riley looked uncertain as to what her response should be.

Dakota turned back to Justus, and he couldn't help but notice how pale her face was beneath her stitches. "Can you take me back to Serenity Shores?"

"Sure." He opened the door for her and then hurried to grab her crutches from the corner. But she had already made her excuses to Reece and Marie and limped halfway out of the restaurant before he could say his goodbyes and catch up to her. He followed her until they were outside under the portico and then took her elbow and forced her to stop. "Here." He held first one crutch and then the other as she settled them beneath her arms, all the while closely watching her face.

She didn't protest. Didn't smile. Didn't meet his gaze. Just slumped against the props as if the life had suddenly drained from her.

He touched her chin and she did look up then, her blue eyes soft and full of some emotion he couldn't quite lay a name to, but it was one full of hurt, pain, and confusion. He allowed his thumb to linger on her chin, stroking softly. He wanted to press for details. What had happened in the couple minutes she'd been out on the deck with Riley? But all he said was, "Stay here and I'll bring the car to you?"

She offered an almost imperceptible nod.

All the way back to Serenity Shores she remained quiet, studying the scenery out her window. One hand pleated and unpleated a section of material in her skirt.

The gravel from the long drive that led down to the main house crunched beneath their tires as he slowly eased the car to a stop in the circular drive. He hurried around to her side of the car to help her out. When she stood, he gripped her shoulders. "Do you want to talk about it, now?"

She rolled her lips inward and mashed them together, looking toward the ocean that lay in the dark somewhere below the bluff they were on. "I just need some time." She brushed past him and her crutches clunked along the walk that led around the side of the house toward the back patio.

He shoved his keys into his pocket. He should leave her be. Only a little bit ago he'd been telling Jalen the same thing. Leave me alone, I need time. But something wouldn't let him go up to his room as though everything were alright. He went inside, drank some water at the kitchen sink, more to kill time than because he was thirsty, and then propped his hands against the counter and leaned there trying to decide what to do. A gentleman would probably leave her alone as she'd asked. But he couldn't do it. He clunked his cup onto the granite and strode purposefully through the living room to the slider that led out back.

It took a moment for him to find her.

Dakota sat on the flat-top stone fence that rimmed the upper tier of the backyard, curled up into a little ball with her arms wrapped around her knees and her body rocking slightly. It was probably her body language – so similar to that of Treyvon's after he'd killed Helene – that sent his heart rate skyrocketing.

He sank down beside her and rested one hand on her shoulder. "Talk to me."

He felt even more terrified when, instead of responding, Dakota simply turned and curled into his chest, wrapping her arms around him. He could feel her trembling, but she wasn't crying, and she didn't say a word.

Justus swallowed the lump in his throat. His palm smoothed over the long silken strands of her hair. Below them the ocean sang its constant repetitive melody. "What can I do for you?"

She shook her head. Sniffed. Then said softly, "Earlier I told you about the wreck I was in. The man in the pickup? I just found out he was Riley's boyfriend."

Justus's eyes dropped closed and he rested his chin against her head.

"She said he...became so abusive after the wreck." A tremor shivered through her.

Justus felt all the air rush from his lungs, and he held her a little tighter. Dakota thought Riley's situation was her fault. And boy, didn't he know what that felt like, he suddenly realized. Somehow even though his head knew it wasn't his fault – what happened to Helene – his heart wanted to find some assignment for the blame. "Don't do this to yourself. What that man did to her, you can't hold yourself responsible for that."

She only sniffled and held her silence.

And then he was pouring out Treyvon's story to her. Laying bare all the emotions he'd felt from responsibility, to guilt, to horror and anger, and how he wasn't sure he would ever be able to run Deschutes Rejuvenation with the same passion as before. "I thought I'd reached him. Helped him change. But he hit her with a baseball bat in an argument over a shopping trip she took."

She listened quietly as he laid the whole story out and worked through the tangled knots of his emotions. "In the end I've had to realize that I did the best I could to reach him and he rejected what I had to say. Rejected God. As much as that hurts, I can't believe his actions are my fault." When he finally stopped talking and eased out the first breath of relief he'd felt in weeks, she still said nothing.

He leaned back from her and took her face in both his hands.

Moonlight shimmered in the moist blue of her eyes. She searched his face as though needing every scrap of truth and comfort he might have to offer, and he let her look.

After a long moment he spoke softly. "His reaction to the accident is not your responsibility. You can't take that on yourself. Trust me, I know." *And wouldn't Jalen love to hear me say it.*

She blinked slowly. "I guess I know that," she touched her temple, "but here," she rested a hand against her heart, "it hurts too much to let it go."

"I know that too." So much emotion welled up in him at that moment. He wanted, no *needed*, to protect this woman from all the pain life was throwing at her.

Before he realized what he was doing, his lips had settled against her forehead. The smooth softness of her skin and the little gasp she let loose tantalized him.

Dakota willed herself to breathe normally as Justus pulled back slightly. What was she doing here? They were hovering, teetering, on the edge of a relationship. Her mind swirled in a crazy mix of desire to jump in head first, and terror at the same prospect.

He studied her for a long minute. Somehow he had the ability to make her acutely aware that she couldn't look her best right now. Not with the bruising and stitches and probably tear-smeared makeup. And yet at the same time she had a feeling none of that mattered to him.

Finally he said, "Can I ask you a question?" His fingers stroked the sleeves of her jacket.

She stilled, and swallowed down the lump that must be her heart in her throat.

His intention shimmered in his eyes before he spoke. "I know we haven't known each other that long—" His jaw bunched as he turned to look out over the water.

Dakota took a slow breath to calm her Benedict Arnold of a pulse and tried to keep from trembling as she waited for him to go on. Not a cloud hung in the sky, and the December breeze was cold. To keep her fingers busy, she reached for her hood.

"Here, let me..." Justus tugged the fur-lined covering into place, cinching it under her chin and tying it.

"Thanks."

He rested his hands on her shoulders, searching her face intently. If anything the intensity in his scrutiny had grown.

She fiddled with the cuffs on her coat and hoped he hadn't felt the tremor that had just coursed through her. The breeze played with his curls, tantalizing her with its freedom to caress through them. It ought to be a crime for any man to look so good. To have such blue eyes that seemed to be able to see into her very soul. She felt her forehead tense up. Why was she letting herself feel these things when she knew it was impossible to let it go anywhere?

Finally he let loose a little breath and a hint of a smile tugged at the corner of his mouth. "I have a bit of a confession."

"Oh?" Had the word sounded as breathy to him as it had to her?

"The night of the storm...I was coming early to ask you out to dinner." He quirked an eyebrow like that should mean something to her.

Her pulse hammered and her mouth was suddenly parched. "But you said—"

He touched a finger to her lips. "I know what I said. But God keeps reminding me lately how short life is. And...I wasn't being quite honest when I said I just wanted to be your friend."

"Oh." She pinched the inside of her lip between her teeth. Forced herself to remain steady and not sway toward him.

She scrabbled to remind herself of the reasons why Justus was not a man she wanted to pursue a relationship with, but all of them suddenly seemed very thin and threadbare.

A man who normally rode everywhere on a motorbike. *That's flimsy and you know it.*

Dangerous job. *But no one is assured tomorrow.*

"So if not just friends, then...?"

He gently touched a strand of her hair that had escaped from her hood. "Go on a date with me? Something light. Dinner. A movie. We'll see where it goes from there." Vulnerability cloaked his features. "I like you a lot, Dakota."

She eased out a slow breath, not ready to admit

to him that the feeling was mutual. And a little bit petrified of just how much she did like him. She eased away and turned to stare down the embankment beside them.

An ex-con... *Heavy on the ex.*

Still... Justus had served time. He'd started Deschutes Rejuvenation to help boys like he had been. And he'd just told her that one of those boys had killed someone! What had Justus done to end up in jail? She felt a wash of lightheadedness. *Dakota, stop it. He obviously didn't kill anyone or he would still be in jail.* Even so...how much did she really know about the man?

"Justus, I need to know..." She folded her arms against the chill, unable to look at him.

"You need to know what?" He leaned in to her line of vision, concern tightening his jawline.

Did she really want to know? And how did one phrase such a question?

She shook away the melancholy and added a little drama to her shiver. "Never mind. It's cold out here, and we have an early morning tomorrow." Her crutches clunked against the wall as she grabbed for them.

Justus sighed, but stood when she did and followed her to the patio door. He opened it and let her step inside, then reached out a hand to stop her from leaving. His gaze drilling into hers, he reached behind himself and slowly pulled the slider shut. "So do I get an answer?"

She wished she'd been able to get away without

having to give him an answer she knew would hurt him. She pretended not to understand. "Did you ask me a question?"

Instead of filling with humor like she'd expected it to, his face turned very serious. "Dakota Trask, will you have dinner with me?"

She swallowed, and rolled her lips in, pressing them together. The scent of his cologne wafted to her, spicy and tantalizing. She took in the soft light of his gaze, and remembered how gentle he'd been with the little boy they'd almost hit. How highly Reece spoke of him. How tender and caring he'd been toward her over the last several days. Not to mention his frequent acknowledgements of God's faithfulness in his life. That last one was huge.

She tried to push aside her concerns. One date. What could it hurt?

It could hurt a lot.

"Justus, I'm sorry. I wish I could say yes, but—" How did a woman tell a man she couldn't date him because he'd been to jail and she didn't know why? No tactful way of saying it came to mind, so she just let the silence hang between them.

Justus rubbed the back of his neck and studied her, a touch of hurt lingering in his eyes. She hated that she'd put it there. Finally, he dropped his hands to his hips and gave a slight nod. "I think I understand."

She rubbed her Adam's apple with the tips of her fingers and turned her attention to the staircase, wishing away the pain that had settled at the base of her throat. "I better head up and get some sleep. I'll see you in the morning."

He turned his back, folded his arms, and settled in to his heels as he stared into the darkness beyond the window. "Yeah. See you then." His expression, reflected in the glass, showed that his eyes had dropped closed.

She wanted to go to him, wrap her arms around him, and tell him it was all a mistake. But her feet dragged her toward the stairs instead.

"Dakota?" His voice stopped her on the bottom tread.

She turned towards him and arched her brows.

"When you are ready to hear the answer, you ask your question. I'll be happy to tell you what you want to know."

Her pulse thundered in her ears and she knew she must look like a wide eyed doe about to be struck by a semi. But she had no rejoinder at the moment. All she said was, "Goodnight, Justus," and resumed her climb of the stairs.

What would her mother and father say if she told them she just might be falling for a man who'd been to prison? She used the handrail to pull herself up the last few steps. One thing was certain. She'd better shore up her defenses and keep her distance from the man, because he'd most definitely found a breach.

With a sigh, she closed her bedroom door behind her and leaned against it. She needed more Tylenol if she was going to be able to sleep. Her headache was coming on strong again.

Justus entered his room and fell back on the bed, clasping his hands behind his head. He'd seen the questions in her eyes. And he'd wanted to tell her. But she needed to be ready to hear. He didn't want his story to sound like a plea for her sympathy. And that thought alone had kept the words dammed up inside him.

When she was ready she would ask. Cold terror, mixed with anticipation, washed through him at that prospect. Really what did he have to lose? His time-served hung between them already. He knew what he'd been, and it wasn't pretty. Not even close. He also knew that when she learned the truth about what had put him in jail, she would see him a little differently. That might be good. That thought had tempted him to blurt the whole story tonight. But he didn't want her thinking he was telling her only to get her commiseration. No pity-dates for him, thank you very much.

He sat up slowly and pulled off his shoes, then headed into the bathroom to brush his teeth. As he brushed, he stared at himself in the mirror. He looked pathetic and miserable. He grunted and propped both hands against the sink with his head bowed and the water still running.

God, help me to put this in Your hands. And help me to know where You want me to go from here. And if there's to be an "us", then help me to trust You to work that out too. I could also use some direction on what to do about D.R. I'd like to put my head down and just walk away. Do something easier. But I keep feeling a check every time I think that's what I've decided to do.

He scooped water into his mouth and swished.

Not to mention, when Dakota did see things a little differently after he told her about his past, what then? If he went back to eastern Oregon to run Deschutes Rejuvenation again, would she be willing to come with him? Would he even want to take a woman into that kind of ministry with him? No. No way.

He spat into the sink and blew out a frustrated breath as he slapped off the water and the light. *God, I'm a mess down here.*

Chapter 10

Dakota woke up the morning of the wedding with a splitting headache and a mouth so dry her tongue felt stiff. Dread pressed in. Not today of all days! She eased her eyes open and tested the sunlight streaming through her window. Burning pin pricks bombarded so painfully that she snapped them shut again.

The doctors had said the malaria might come back in six months to a year. And the doctor at the hospital last week had warned that exhaustion could bring it back on. But she'd been feeling fine yesterday other than the slight headache that had plagued her at the end of the rehearsal dinner and into the evening. She hadn't expected it to come back now, not on such an important day, for sure. At least it didn't seem to have come back in full force. Yet.

She groaned and pushed her hands into the mattress, forcing herself to shuffle to her bathroom.

A chill shook her, and she heard her breath

stuttering through her lips. Goose bumps popped up all over her arms. Okay, maybe it was a little worse than she first thought.

She fumbled one hand through the medicine cabinet, forcing her eyes to open to slits. Tylenol and Advil would have to get her through the wedding. Because she wouldn't let Marie down for anything. But she'd put a call in to Doctor Dallas, the local tropical disease specialist, and maybe she could get in to see him tomorrow.

She poured two white pills into her palm and downed them with a chaser of water. Then she crawled back onto her bed and pulled the covers up to her ears. Fifteen minutes. She would hopefully feel a little better in fifteen minutes. After that she'd have to get up and dress or be late for the wedding...

Seemingly only a moment later, knocking on the door jolted her upright. Something had her skull in a vice grip, and she gasped at the force of it. But her eyes felt a little better.

"Dakota, you ready in there? It's time to go." Justus's voice sounded a little worried and still a little dejected.

Her eyes dropped closed as their conversation from the night before invaded.

Then they popped open again! Time to go? A frown puckered her brow. She scooped a hand back through her hair and glanced at her phone on the night stand. Ten fifteen, and five missed calls from Marie and two from Taysia. Alarm shot through her and she leapt off the bed. They were supposed to be at the church in twenty minutes! As fast as her still-tender ankle would allow, she hustled to the door and opened it a crack, peering around it.

Justus's eyes widened as he took in her T-shirt and shorts and what she felt sure was a hairdo to outshine all hairdos.

"I think my malaria is back. But I feel better now. Give me fifteen minutes?"

"Malaria?" He placed a palm on the door to keep her from shutting it. "You should be in bed resting. Marie will understand."

"No! I don't want to let her down. And I don't want to miss it." She gave him an apologetic wince. "I meant to get up earlier. Just think, you'll get to show me what that speedy little red car of yours can actually do. Give me fifteen minutes? I'll be fine." She firmly shut the door in his face and rushed to the bathroom.

Advil. She would take some now as a layer on top of the Tylenol she'd taken earlier.

God, please just get me through this day and help it to be wonderful for Marie and Reece.

Justus paced in the dining room, concern for Dakota tightening his chest. But, true to her word, she appeared at the bottom of the stairs fifteen minutes later.

"You sure you're going to be okay?" Justus

studied her carefully.

Her face was a little peaked and there were slight bags under her red eyes, but other than that she looked beautiful. So good, in fact, his concern was momentarily forgotten and he swallowed hard.

Dakota's navy blue bridesmaid dress was a sleek sheath of velvet with a flare around the ankles. Sapphire blue gems studded one shoulder and swept down to Dakota's waist.

"I'll be fine. Just get us to the church." She hurried towards him.

He stopped her. "You'll need a coat?"

"Oh." She put one hand to her forehead. "I forgot. I'll just run up and—"

"No. Don't. Here." He swept off his own leather jacket and settled it around her shoulders. Taking up his suit coat which hung over the back of one of the dining room chairs, he slipped it on. "This will work just fine for me. Let's go."

He took the roads as quickly as he could without getting a ticket, and tried not to worry too much as Dakota called to make an appointment with a tropical diseases doctor.

"This afternoon? Oh no, I can't come in today—"

He settled one hand against her knee. "Yes. Yes, you can. I'll take you."

"Oh, well, actually, yes I'll take it. Four thirty. Yes. I'll be there. Thank you." She hung up and tilted her head back against the headrest. Her eyes dropped closed and she didn't even seem to have the energy to look at him when she said, "You've already done so much for me, I hate to ask you to do more. I'm cleared to drive now. But I'll just need you to give me a ride back to the house to get my car."

"You may be cleared to drive, but I'm not letting you drive yourself anywhere in your condition. I don't mind taking you at all."

"It might take a while. Sometimes it takes a long time to get the blood work back from the lab."

"It will be fine." He grinned at her, intent on lightening her mood. "Maybe when you see what a helpful guy I can be you'll agree to that first date."

Her lips thinned into what could have been taken for a smile if it wasn't so weary around the edges. "If my picture is by 'pigheaded' in the dictionary, yours must be next to persistent."

He chuckled. "Maybe it is, at that." He pulled up to a spot directly in front of the church's double doors. "You get out here, and I'll meet you inside."

She gave him an appreciative smile. "You're a lifesaver."

"If I was any kind of lifesaver you'd be home sound asleep in your bed."

She pulled herself from the car and cocked one eyebrow at him. "That would be nice, but Marie is worth it."

He nodded. "Reece is too. Without him and Jalen I don't know if Deschutes Rejuvenation would have even gotten off the ground. If you wait for me inside, I'll walk you down."

Dakota leaned one shoulder into the foyer wall, relieved to note that her layering of acetaminophen and ibuprofen seemed to be working. She was bone weary, but she would make it through.

Justus entered only a moment later and Dakota hurried with him to the room where the bridesmaids were to wait. "See you in a few." He squeezed her elbow and headed across the hall to the groomsmen's room.

"Oh, you're here!" When Marie saw her walk in, she looked like a frazzled mother of toddling triplets whose husband had just arrived home from work.

Dakota apologized profusely and explained what had happened.

"I'm so sorry." Marie pulled her into a quick hug. "Are you sure you're going to be okay? You don't have to do this."

Dakota nodded. "Yes, I'll be fine. Really." She glanced around. "Where's Riley?"

"She's downstairs helping Darlene put the finishing touches on the reception hall."

Dakota eyed Marie. "How are you doing? Did you eat something?"

Marie nodded. "Darlene made me coffee, eggs and toast before I ever left the house. And she brought me apple slices and cheese a little bit ago."

Dakota slipped off the comforting cocoon of Justus's jacket and accepted the bouquet Taysia thrust into her hands with a smile. "Thanks for filling in for me." A wave of chills gripped her at the loss of warmth, and goose bumps speckled her arms.

Taysia gave her arm a squeeze. "No problem. Sorry you aren't feeling well."

Marie stepped forward and took both of their hands. "Would you two mind if we prayed?"

Dakota immediately felt a touch of relief in her spirit. Prayer might be the only thing that would get her through this ceremony. "I'd love that."

A knock sounded on the door and the pastor's wife poked her head in. "It's time, ladies! The photographer is waiting for you all in the sanctuary."

Marie's eyes sparkled with excitement as she nodded then spun back to them. "Okay, *quick* prayer. Taysia, maybe you could lead us?" The sparkle turned to a sheen of moisture.

Taysia gave her a side hug. "Of course. I'd love to." And she launched in. She prayed for Marie to have peace, for her and Reece's relationship to be built on the solid foundation of God's Word. She prayed for Riley – that their love for her and for Jesus would lead her to a relationship with Him. And she concluded with a quick prayer for Dakota to feel better and make it through the ceremony.

The photographer obviously knew what she was doing and made the photo session seem like a breeze. And then it was time, and Dakota and Justus were walking down the aisle arm in arm.

Dakota had always loved December weddings.

And even though she'd seen it all yesterday, she took it in again with new appreciation. Two large trees stood on each side of the podium. White lights and deep burgundy poinsettias added a comforting splash of color to the room. The aisle was also lined with lights and poinsettia bushes, and the two large bouquets on either side of center were built with red-throated lilies, white roses, and deep green ferns. But the best sight of all was seeing Reece, standing at the head of the aisle, fidgeting like a little boy on Christmas morning. His attention was fixed on the doors behind them, anticipation sparkling in his green eyes as he craned to see around them to the main doors where Marie would appear at any moment.

Justus leaned toward her as they neared the end of the aisle. "You sure you're going to be okay?"

She kept her smile in place and nodded imperceptibly. "I'll be fine. Stop worrying."

"That's not likely to happen anytime today," he mumbled as he escorted her to her place on the platform and then took his position on the other side.

Dakota willed away the goose bumps that threatened to return and forced her attention to the back doors as the bridal processional started up and Marie swept in with Alyssa looking proud as punch by her side. It had been Reece's idea to have Alyssa escort Marie up the aisle because Marie's father was still serving time for a B&E he'd committed.

Serving time. Dakota's gaze darted across the

platform to Justus. She could cross "breaking and entering" off her list, she supposed. He'd likely still be in if he'd done something that serious. Except he would have been a juvenile and likely would have gotten a lesser sentence. So maybe it was still an option. She sighed. Why hadn't she just asked him last night?

She suddenly realized Justus had caught her staring and jerked her focus back to the couple just meeting at the head of the aisle.

"Who gives this woman to be married to this man?" the pastor asked.

"I do!" Alyssa's chest puffed out even more, if that were possible.

Despite the pain suddenly burning in all her joints, Dakota grinned, and the whole sanctuary rippled with humor.

Marie bent and kissed Alyssa on the cheek and then the little girl dashed over and clambered up on the bench next to Reece's mom. "Did I do good, Grandma?" she asked in a very non-inside voice.

Another wave of laughter rolled through the room.

Marie covered her mouth, a little embarrassment tinting her cheeks pink.

As Darlene shushed Alyssa with grandmotherly affection, Reece chuckled and pulled Marie to his side. When Marie and Reece took the three steps to stand before the minister on the platform, Dakota moved down to the main floor of the sanctuary, pulled in a slow breath with dread at needing to use any joint, and bent to adjust Marie's short train. When she stood, a wave of light headedness drained through her, but it only took a moment and a quick shake of her head to set her back to rights. She resumed her spot and accepted her bouquet from Taysia. She could feel Justus's gaze drilling into her.

She chose not to look over. It would hurt her neck too much and only add fuel to his fire of worry.

The ceremony was short, with only one song to interrupt the vows, and soon Justus's warm hand had settled over hers where she rested it in the crook of his arm, and they were following the happy couple back down the aisle.

By the time they reached the foyer however, Dakota's legs were trembling so badly they were in danger of giving out, and it had nothing to do with the fact that she'd been gimping around on crutches for the past several days. Her eyes felt like a tailor had mistaken them for a pin cushion and were watering unstoppably.

Justus led her to a chair and thrust a handful of tissues from a nearby box into her hands. "Wait here, I'll get my jacket and your purse, but I'm taking you to the hospital right now." He was gone before she could protest.

Dakota dabbed at her tear ducts and held her breath as pain vibrated through every knuckle in her hand and her eye felt set afire with each dab of the tissue. She'd have loved nothing more than to tell him she had other obligations, but the truth was she couldn't find the energy. Couldn't have found the energy if she was paid. She kept her eyes closed and tipped her head back against the wall. Maybe if she just rested for a moment.

But Justus was back before she even had the chance to do that. "Hey, you ready?" He nudged her upward and slid the wonderful warmth of his jacket around her shoulders. "Let's get you to the hospital."

"But the dance—"

"—don't worry about the dance." Marie was there by her side, with Reece looking concerned too. "Just get better."

Dakota wanted to cry, but couldn't deny a measure of relief. "I'm so sorry."

Marie squeezed her shoulder and Dakota gritted her teeth to keep from crying out. "I just wish I'd known you were so sick. You never should have had to stand through the ceremony."

Forcing a smile she hoped looked real, Dakota tried to reassure them. "I was fine really."

"But you're not right now. Let's go." Justus held one hand toward the exit.

"Congrats, you two," Dakota called over her shoulder as she preceded Justus toward the door.

Marie curled into Reece's side and looked up at him. "Thanks."

There was so much love in her expression, and in Reece's as he looked back down at his new wife, that Dakota felt the awe of it. And as she stood just inside the doors waiting for Justus to run get the car, she wanted only one thing.

Someday I want a relationship with someone who will love me like Reece loves Marie, Lord.

The only problem was, the man who sprang to mind came with too many risks and not enough guarantees.

Chapter 11

A little bit of terror danced in Justus's chest.

The minute he'd opened the car door for Dakota back at the church, she'd sunk into the seat, punched the heater button, and curled into a little ball with her eyes closed. Every once in a while she moaned softly, but he couldn't tell if she was asleep or just in so much pain she couldn't help herself.

He knew one thing for sure as he pulled into the hospital's emergency room parking lot, his heartrate hadn't been this high since the night Treyvon had killed his girlfriend. Justus eased the car to a stop under the emergency room portico and hopped out. He dashed around and opened her door. "Come on, Dakota. We're here."

A low groan and a shudder were her only response.

He skimmed a hand over her forehead. She was burning up! She needed help, and she needed it now. He glanced around. There was nothing for it but to leave her here for a second and run inside to get someone.

He left the car idling and jogged through the sliding glass doors to the triage counter. No attendant was in sight. Of course not. He could hear a bevy of activity happening through a door just behind the desk and pressed the bell on the counter to call someone to come. But no one emerged and he needed to at least get Dakota inside where it was warm.

A wheelchair sat empty near the wall. He snagged it and hurried back to the car, only to find Dakota pulling herself out already, and trying to lean down inside the car to get her purse. Her knees wobbled like a newborn giraffe. "Whoa." He lurched toward her and guided her fall into the wheelchair. Then grabbed her purse and set it on her lap. She whimpered and murmured something about fire. He touched her forehead again. If she was feeling even half as warm internally it was no wonder fire was on her mind.

He swung around to wheel her inside, but a scrub clad woman strode out the doors looking all businesslike. "I've got her sir, thank you. What are her symptoms?" She held up a hand for him to stop.

Justus gladly relinquished control of the wheelchair to the nurse, even if he was wondering where she'd been only a moment ago. "She thinks she has malaria. She's had it before. But her fever just spiked in the last few minutes."

"Okay," the woman carefully guided the wheelchair toward the entrance. "I need you to park your car. You can't leave it there." She walked calmly, more like she was out for a Sunday stroll than wheeling a very sick woman into an emergency room.

He ignored the comment and stepped out ahead of her, hoping to hurry her up a bit. His car could get towed for all he cared. They would need paperwork filled out, likely.

The nurse stopped still. When he spun back to see why, her eyebrows arched and she tipped her head in the direction of his still idling Z3. Her lips pursed like a perturbed mother.

Could the woman show any *less* concern? His gaze dropped to Dakota. Her eyes remained closed and her face was red and blotchy. "She's really sick."

"Yes, sir. We'll get her taken care of. Feel free to come inside after you've parked your car."

An ambulance pulled in just behind him at that moment, lights flashing. The nurse quickly put the brake on Dakota's chair and pointed him once more to his car as she hurried toward the ambulance.

Dakota looked up at him through squinted eyes. "I'll be fine. Just go."

Torn between staying with Dakota and getting out of the ambulance's way, Justus gave in to the inevitable. "I'll only be a second." He jogged back to park the car. It took driving down two rows to find a spot and when he finally dashed across the parking lot, Dakota still sat curled over in the wheelchair exactly in the place the nurse had left her, her head propped in her hands. "You've got to be kidding me!"

The ambulance was gone, presumably along with the ER nurse. Dakota had apparently been demoted on the triage list. But they could at least have taken her inside! Just as he was about to step off the curb to cross to her, a red Civic peeled into the drop off zone, going way too fast for a hospital parking lot. Justus pinwheeled his arms to keep from landing in its path.

At that moment a flash of color behind Dakota caught his attention. A little body darted out from behind a bush near the emergency room entrance, making a beeline for Dakota.

What in the world—

The metallic red car screeched to a halt right in front of him under the ER portico and a man lurched out. "I've got you, honey, just hold on!"

Justus craned to see Dakota beyond the man's shoulder.

The kid snatched Dakota's purse and kept sprinting.

"Stop!" Justus lurched forward. He and the man from the car nearly collided near the trunk of the little red coupe.

"Watch it, buddy, we're having a baby here!"

"Sorry." Justus spun to avoid a full on collision with the man who was still darting for his wife's door, tossed a glance at Dakota to make sure she was still doing okay, and then took off in full pursuit of the boy who was just disappearing around the corner and headed toward the street.

The boy was quick, but Justus was quicker and within several strides he had the little purse snatcher held aloft by his collar.

Dakota's purse tumbled to the pavement and the boy grabbed on to Justus's arm, kicking and hollering. "Let me go!"

The familiar voice snapped Justus to attention. "Wait a minute!" He set the boy down and spun him around, gripping his shoulders firmly. "You?"

The boy kicked out and his toe connected solidly with Justus's shin.

Justus grunted and on reflex let the kid go, but the boy only got two steps away before Justus had him firmly in grasp again.

It was the same boy he and Dakota had almost run over the other day. His red hair stood from his head in tangled patches and his freckles sharply contrasted with his pale face. "I didn't mean any harm, mister, honest I didn't." The boy squirmed, trying to free himself.

But eight years of working with troubled youth had taught Justus a thing or two about keeping hold of one when he wanted to without hurting him. "Didn't mean any harm, but you snatched a sick woman's purse?" Another wave of pain shot up his leg. "And kicked me?"

At least the kid had the decency to hang his head.

Across the street a group of laughing teen boys drew his attention. They kept glancing his way and then dissolving into another fit of laughter and back slapping. Justus would bet his bottom dollar the boy, who was dressed in designer clothes and didn't look like he'd gone without necessities a day in his life, had been dared to snatch the purse.

Justus kept a firm hold on him as he bent down and retrieved Dakota's bag. "You're not going anywhere until we can talk to the cops, but first I need to help my friend. So you're coming with me." He marched the kid back toward the emergency room entrance.

Some chord of familiarity begged for his attention. It wasn't that he'd seen the kid before so much as that he reminded him of someone. That same ring of familiarity had been there the first time he'd seen the kid too. Who was it the kid reminded him of? He couldn't quite put his finger on it.

Thankfully Dakota was no longer sitting in the wheelchair outside the entrance. Hopefully she was not only inside but was being taken care of.

In his relief, he relaxed his grip.

Like a slippery fish on an unbarbed hook, the boy twisted with lightning speed and darted away again.

Justus rolled his eyes. The boy didn't have a chance against his long stride. "You're not making this easy, kid." Justus wrapped one hand firmly around the boy's upper arm, bringing him once more to a halt.

This time he wasn't taking any chances. He detoured to his car. Popping the trunk, he pulled out his Oregon Juvenile Justice badge and the set of handcuffs he kept inside. How many times over the years had he had some kid handcuffed to his wrist to keep track of him? He'd lost count. But when he ratcheted the lock into place around the boy's wrist and then did the same to his own, the boy's eyes widened and filled with unshed tears. This was obviously a first for the kid. Good, maybe this would teach him a well-earned lesson.

"My dad will take you to court."

Justus almost felt sorry for him. "Actually, reasonable suspicion is all I need to detain you until the police can get here. And you and I both know I have a lot more than reasonable suspicion."

"This is child abuse! You can't do this, Mister!"

Justus's lips thinned. "I just did. And if you had any idea how many times a kid has said that to me... You don't think what you did to that woman was abuse? She's sick and vulnerable, and you take advantage of her? You know what?" He pointed to the surveillance equipment in the corner of the portico. "There is going to be video footage of you. Did you ever think about that?"

The kid's face paled and he looked a little startled at that thought.

When Justus strode back into the emergency room, Angry-Mom-Nurse looked up from behind the triage desk. "Oh, your wife is in the back..." Her words trailed away as her gaze settled on the shiny links connecting his wrist to the boy's.

Justus dropped Dakota's purse on the counter

and flashed the nurse his badge. It really wasn't anything more than proof that he was certified as an Oregon juvenile detention agent, but he hoped it would keep questions to a minimum.

He tipped a nod from the boy to the purse. "He stole her purse. I'm a correctional officer and will be keeping track of him till the police can come. How is she?"

The nurse was slightly bug-eyed. "She's in the back being looked at by a doctor now."

"Good. First, she's not my wife. Second, she has a tropical disease specialist she was supposed to see this afternoon at four thirty. I don't remember his name. But I didn't think she should wait that long. Can you please see that she gets this purse while I deal with the kid?"

The woman nodded slowly and picked up the bag.

"Thanks." Justus dropped one hand against the boy's shoulder. "Now, let's have a little talk, shall we, before I call the police."

The boy swallowed visibly.

"What's your name, kid?"

The boy's eyes narrowed and his jaw jutted off to one side. He refused to meet Justus's gaze and tried to affect an indifferent stance by folding his arms, but was brought up short with the reminder that one of his wrists was cuffed to Justus.

"Okay, so you don't want to tell me your name. Fine. I'll just call you Kid. How about you tell me why you snatched my friend's purse, *Kid*?" He deliberately put a little emphasis on the last word.

"I don't got to say nothin' to you."

"Fair enough." Justus scrubbed the back of his neck, trying to figure out how he was going to stall long enough to have Kylen be the one who showed up. Right now Kylen would still be at the wedding. To give himself time to think, he propelled the little thief across the waiting room to the vending machine. "You hungry?" He put in a dollar and punched in the number for a Snickers bar.

The boy eyed him like he might be half crazy. "First you cuff me and now you offer me candy?"

Justus shrugged and took a big bite of his candy bar. "Figure we might as well make our time together as pleasant as possible."

"Fine. I'll take the Junior Mints." He shuffled his feet and wore an expression that said he half expected Justus to laugh and tell him it had been a joke.

What kind of a home had this kid been raised in? Justus nodded and inserted another dollar. "Good choice."

When the boy had his Junior Mints, Justus led him back across the room to two chairs that were empty near one corner. He was itching to check on Dakota, but something told him that maybe he'd been brought to this time and place for a reason other than just helping her.

The kid plopped into one of the chairs with a sullen curse. "Call the cops already." His box of candy remained untouched.

Justus took a leisurely bite of his chocolate and sank casually into the chair next to Mr. Personality. "All in good time."

"Creep! You can't keep me chained to your wrist forever, you know. My parents are going to be wondering where I am!"

Kid, they should have been wondering about your whereabouts long before now. "Your parents...who are they?"

The boy huffed, and for a minute Justus thought he wasn't going to answer, but then he blurted, "People you should be afraid of, that's who. My dad is going to go off on you when he learns about this, man." Another string of curses followed as the boy tried to emphasize how scared Justus should be of his father.

"I think I liked you better when you were scared spitless because I'd almost just run over you."

Sadly, the kid might be right about his parents' reaction, but what the little punk didn't know was that Justus had faced down, and lived to tell about, parents who were much scarier than his father likely was. In fact, in the long run, most parents ended up thanking him for the changes he helped foster in their children.

The nurse approached from across the way. "I thought you should know that Doctor Dallas happened to be on campus and is in with Dakota now. And," her lips pressed into a thin line as though she couldn't fathom a reason for her next words, "Dakota is asking for you."

Justus saw another opportunity to stall in calling the cops. "Good. The kid here has something to say to Dakota, anyhow."

The boy rolled his eyes. "No I don't."

Justus sighed, took hold of the half-size villain's arm, and stood. Someone had better get a hold of this kid real soon or his attitude was going to lead him down all kinds of troubling paths.

"Come on, Kid, don't make this harder than it has to be."

With a begrudging grunt, young Mister Purloin dragged his feet beside Justus as they followed the nurse to Dakota's room.

She lay under the covers, her hospital bed tipped up slightly and her face looking pale against the pillows. Her fine blonde hair splayed all around her. But her eyes opened when she heard them enter and she seemed a little more lucid than she'd been a few minutes earlier. A bag of what he presumed was saline and hopefully fever reducer dripped down a tube into her arm.

Her gaze flickered from him to the boy. "I thought someone took my purse. Was I dreaming?"

At the raspy quality of her voice, concern made his insides go soft. "I'm afraid not. But I got it back."

She took in the boy by his side and her brow furrowed. "Isn't he—?"

"Yep. Same kid. In fact, he has something he'd like to say to you." He pegged the kid with his sternest look and raised his brows.

The kid only shuffled his feet and glowered at

the floor. "Told you I got nothin' to say."

In that moment Justus wished he had the right to give the kid's skull a good rapping. Especially since a troubled look tightened Dakota's face.

Instead of manhandling the kid, he leaned over Dakota and brushed a lock of hair from her forehead. He spoke to get her mind off the boy's unrepentant attitude. "How are you feeling?"

Her nose wrinkled. "Better now that the pain meds are kicking in."

"Good. I was really worried about you. Just rest. I'll be right here if you need anything."

She sighed and nestled a little deeper into her pillow. Her eyes dropped closed and she murmured. "I kept trying to figure out who he looks like. It's Riley."

Next to him, the boy jolted as if he'd been stuck with a pin. Justus rubbed his jaw and studied the scrawny red head. That was what he'd been seeing. Yes. The kid really did resemble Riley.

Justus pulled him over to one corner of Dakota's room and kept his voice low. "Riley Ross...Do you know her?"

The kid couldn't have looked more dumbstruck if Justus had announced that he was an alien from outer space. But he recovered even if he did stumble over his words. "I-I don't h-have any idea wh-who you are talking about."

Justus eased out a breath. Riley's brother? Most likely. He was even more glad now that he'd waited till he could talk to Kylen and not just dump the kid into the system. He glanced at his watch. It had been a little over an hour since he and Dakota had left the wedding. The reception was likely winding down. Maybe Kylen could find time to talk to him for a few minutes.

He slipped his phone from his pocket and pressed on Kylen's number.

While he listened to it ring, he removed the cuff from his own wrist and ratcheted it around the arm of a chair, motioning for the kid to sit. With a grumble and a roll of his eyes, he plopped into the seat and then snapped his head back against the wall.

Satisfied that his charge wasn't going anywhere for the time being, Justus stepped into the hallway.

"Hello?" Kylen finally answered.

Justus filled him in quietly. "Better bring Riley too. I think she might know him."

The sound of a vacuum whirred in the background. "Okay. We're almost done here and will be there as soon as we can. Marie and Reece just left to catch their flight, and Taysia's cleaning up."

Slipping his phone back into his pocket, Justus returned to the room. Dakota was sound asleep and breathing deeply. The kid had been crying but swiped madly at his cheeks. Justus gave him his dignity and strode to Dakota's side as though to check on her.

Lord, help me to reach this kid.

The prayer stopped him. How many times had

he prayed that prayer for one boy or another over the years? Too many to count. And how many had he reached? Far fewer than he would have liked. But God hadn't called him to share the gospel so long as it "worked." The call was simply to share.

He looked at the woman lying in the bed and swallowed. It was probably a good thing she'd turned him down for that date. Because he suddenly knew what his answer was. He couldn't abandon his ministry to the boys God kept entrusting to his care. He'd be going back to work at Deschutes Rejuvenation just as soon as his vacation time was up at the end of the week. And – the image of Helene's wide staring eyes flashed into his mind and he shuddered – he couldn't take a woman into that ministry with him.

Relief mingled with sadness as he crossed the room and sank into the chair next to the angry adolescent. Maybe his own story would get through to him. He glanced once more at Dakota. She was still asleep so he didn't need to fear her overhearing. He wanted her to hear this only when she was ready. He had so much remorse for all the pain he'd caused others in the past. He didn't want to cause more with the telling of it.

He leveled his gaze on the boy. "When I was just a few years older than you I served four years of jail time."

The boy's eyebrows went up and he looked over, curiosity apparently overriding his desire to look like he didn't care.

"Want me to tell you why? Forget that." Justus shook his head. "Let me tell you why." He took the still unopened box of Junior Mints from the kid, opened the top, and handed it back. "I grew up in a small town in Oregon a lot like Marinville. When I was fifteen my father, who was a sawyer, worked for a logging outfit. A tree he was falling snapped back on him. Widow Makers they call them." Justus tipped his head against the wall. "Good name for them, I guess, because that's exactly what that tree made of my mother. She went to work full time and then some. And I went to work full time being angry at God."

The boy snorted. "God don't exist, Mister."

Justus chose to ignore that and went on. "There was a group of guys in town that weren't worth much. They were reprobates who did nothing but cause trouble and disrespected everyone, but I decided I wanted to be one of them. Mother was busy working two jobs and didn't notice that I was gone from home most of the time. We did stupid stuff. Tipped over porta johns during the town fair, spray painted our sign all over town, and dared each other to jack loot from the local supermarket."

The kid wiggled in his chair but otherwise held his silence.

"Pretty soon though, those things didn't hold the excitement they once had. We started doing drugs and stealing booze."

The kid rolled his eyes. "Jump to the part where you're in jail. I like that part."

Justus grinned. He liked this kid's spunk. Channeled in the right direction, God could do a lot with it. But as his thoughts turned back to his story, all humor faded.

He rubbed his palms against his knees. "On the corner of First and Pine, old Mr. McKettrick ran McKettrick's Convenience Store. Mick's we called it. First day back after spring break, the boys and I decided to skip school and hit up Mick's for some fun. He had a whole aisle of booze and we figured he'd be easier to get past than the security cameras down at Safeway."

Justus closed his eyes, wishing he could will away the images that always came with the telling of this story. How many boys had he told it to over the years? But the images always remained, and in some ways that was a good thing. Because in the end the incident had been his salvation.

"Mr. McKettrick wasn't the naïve old man we all thought he'd be, however. He'd served his country sneaking through the jungles of Vietnam and then had been on the police force in town for years. He knew a thing or two about delinquents." Justus swiped a hand over his face. "It was my job to chat up Mick while the other guys each made off with a bottle of booze. But before any of my buddies could even make it halfway to the door, old Mick pulled out a sawed-off shotgun he kept under the counter. He just laid it on the laminate next to the register sort of casual like and cleared his throat. The spread on that piece would have covered half the store and we all knew it. But one of the guys – Marshall was his name – had already had a few drinks that morning. Where the rest of us would have just hightailed it out of there, Marshal decided the risk was worth it. He told Mr. McKettrick that he was going to walk out the door with his bottle of Jack Daniels and the old man could come and stop him if he thought he could. Mick grabbed up his sawed-off and before any of us could even think to blink he was around that counter and had it pressed right into Marshall's chest."

Beside Justus, the kid's eyes were as wide as Justus felt sure his had been that day.

"I felt frozen to the spot, wondering what Marshall would do. Marshall wasn't backing down and old Mr. McKettrick had done his fair share of killing and it seemed he didn't want to add one more to his list. After a bit of yelling they finally stood just staring at each other. I was so fixated on hoping Marshall wasn't going to do something really stupid and get himself killed that I didn't even see David. He and Tom were the other guys who had snagged bottles of booze. David ran up behind Mick and broke his bottle over the old man's head." Justus ground his teeth, but then forced himself to finish the tale. "Mick's gun went off out of reflex and Marshall never had a chance as close as the weapon was to his chest. So there's Mick lying on the ground groaning and holding his head, and Marshall is dead and we all know it. And all of us are just staring from them to each other."

The telling of this tale never grew any easier. Justus pulled in a long breath and then let it out slowly.

Silence lingered until the kid prompted, "How'd you get arrested?"

Justus rubbed his palms together. "We heard the sirens then. Mick had pressed a silent alarm at some point, he told me later. Tom and David, they took off like lightning and I intended to be right on their heels. But then as I started to jump over Mr. McKettrick I noticed that not all the blood on the floor was coming from Marshall. Some of it was from a bad laceration on the back of Mick's bald head. I knew if I walked out that door the cops wouldn't get there in time to save him." Justus shrugged. "I took off my shirt and did my best to stop the bleeding and that's where the cops found me. Turned out Mick had surveillance cameras none of us knew about and the whole incident was caught on tape."

"Did the other two get caught?"

Justus nodded. "All of us were convicted. David's still in. Tom got out just a year or two after I did. But you know what the kicker is? Mr. McKettrick came to visit me every month while I was in jail. That man had more forgiveness in him than anyone I'd ever known. He talked to me about how bitter he'd been when he got home from 'Nam. And then he started telling me about Jesus and how his life had changed after he started serving God."

The kid huffed at that.

Justus settled one hand on the small bony

shoulder and undid the top two buttons on his shirt, then pulled it aside. The boy's eyes found the tattoo just below his collarbone and over his heart. It was a simple one – "Mick" in small capped letters.

The boy shrugged off his hand and smirked. "You got the old man's name tatted on your chest?"

Justus readjusted his shirt as he nodded. "Because of his relationship with Jesus, Mick was able to love me in a way that shook me to my core. My mom had taken me to Sunday school when I was little, but I'd always dismissed it as mostly a fairy tale. But because of Mick's example, I eventually realized that wasn't true and gave my life over to God too, and now you know what I do? I help boys, many of whom are just like I was. Mixed up in the wrong crowd, just trying to be somebody, when in reality they already *are* somebody if they would just begin to see themselves as God sees them."

The boy slumped back in his chair and looked away.

Justus sighed. "I don't know what all you are mixed up in, but I do know you are hanging with the wrong crowd. And I can promise you it will only lead you to trouble."

The kid held his silence.

"You ever heard of Jesus?"

Another snort. "Hasn't everyone?"

"You might be surprised. I've given you a lot to think about today, but I'll end with this. Jesus is not just some fairy tale. He's real. And He loves you more than you can imagine."

A sound of disgust escaped the boy's lips. "Loves me enough to send me to jail, you mean?"

Justus ruffled one hand over the mop of red hair. "If that's what it takes. It's what it took for me."

Movement from the bed drew Justus's attention and he glanced over. Everything in him froze. Dakota was looking right at him, tears shimmering in her eyes and tracking back into her hair.

He swallowed. How much of that story had she heard? He took in her tears. Obviously enough that she was distraught.

Regret filled him. He stood and stepped toward her, but at that moment Kylen knocked on the door and poked his head inside.

Justus felt a helpless sense of futility. Maybe he and Dakota were simply not meant to have this conversation. He rubbed one hand back over his head and gestured for Kylen to come inside. His questions and explanations would have to wait.

Chapter 12

With Jalen on her heels, Riley strode purposefully through the door after Kylen, her heart in her throat. Kylen had said Justus felt she might know the boy he had caught stealing Dakota's purse. And if he was right—

She froze in her tracks so quickly that Jalen bumped into her from behind. His hands slid up her arms to cup her shoulders and he squeezed her gently and nudged her forward. That was all the encouragement she needed to find her voice. "Remington Dylan Ross, why are you not in school?"

Her little brother smirked. "What do you care? You haven't been by the house in months!" His gaze flickered over her face and down to her cast and then he swallowed and fiddled with the silver bracelet around his wrist. "You look better."

Better was relative. The last time she'd seen him had been several weeks ago at Nate's funeral. Only a few days after Nate had beaten her up and then driven himself off a cliff. Before that she'd been busy surviving. So Rem's accusation was true enough.

She turned the ire of her emotions onto Justus. "You handcuffed him? He's twelve years old!"

Justus didn't look a bit remorseful. He only folded his arms and leaned back into his heels. "He's old enough to steal a purse? He's old enough to wear some silver. I wouldn't have had to cuff him if he'd been cooperating. So I take it he's not homeschooled?"

That last question almost made her laugh. She shook her head. "No." And the part about the cuffs was probably right, she supposed. She took a breath and pinched the bridge of her nose, then directed her words back to her brother. "Where are Mom and Dad?"

He shrugged. "Dad's on business in Europe somewhere. Mom's around."

Riley's fingernails bit into her palms. By "around" he probably meant she was alone and never far from the wet bar for half of each night and dead-drunk asleep for the other half. "When does Dad get home?"

He sniffed his antipathy. "Who cares?"

She threw up her hands. "You're in a lot of trouble here! You might show a little concern!"

"What do you care?! It's not like you've been falling over yourself to help any! Maybe I needed the money!"

She did bark a laugh then. More to ease her

conscience than at the thought of one of Dylan Ross's children needing money. "That's a good one!"

She thought of the bank account Dad had set up for her when he kicked her out of the house. She hadn't touched it to this day except to remove his name from the account so he wouldn't have access to the money, because she wouldn't put it past him to bleed the account dry just to teach her some sort of twisted lesson.

Remington was still glowering at her.

She snagged her phone from her bag. "Let me just call up Dad and tell him you snatched a purse because you needed some money! Let's see what he says about that."

Rem's eyes widened. "No don't. I'll do the time, or whatever. Just get me away from this Jesus freak"—he tipped his head toward Justus— "and let me get on with my life."

Guilt immediately washed through her. She shouldn't have threatened him with Dad. She of all people knew what it was like to be on Dad's bad side. It was one of the main reasons she rarely went home anymore. And likely the reason Mom had turned to drink. But that didn't give him any reason to disrespect Justus and her friends.

She cuffed his head, and it was a lot more gently than she would have like to. "That 'Jesus Freak' is the only reason you are still sitting here and not already on your way to Juvy where you belong."

"Whatever. They got everything back. It's not like it was a big deal or anything."

Riley threw up her hands and spun away from him before she gave in to the temptation to take her cast to his head.

Across the room Jalen stood with his arms folded, one hand resting against his cheek. He met her gaze, sympathy and understanding cloaking his features. She fisted one hand, wanting to cuss him for his gentle empathy that drew her when she wanted nothing but distance between herself and anyone of the male species for the rest of her life.

Instead, she turned her focus on Kylen. "What now?"

Kylen shrugged. "That depends on if Dakota wants to press charges, or not." All eyes in the room focused on Dakota for a moment before Kylen turned back to her and added, "You'd better call your mother."

"And we all need to get out of here and let Dakota get some rest," Justus added.

Riley glanced over and blinked. Dakota's eyes were red like she'd been crying. Riley narrowed another glare at her brother. These people had been like a breath of fresh air to her since even before Nate's death and she hated that her brother was the cause of some hurt to them, no matter how small. She snapped her fingers at Rem. "Up. Let's go."

He rolled his eyes at her and yanked on the handcuffs to clatter them against the metal of his chair.

If she wasn't mistaken Justus's lips twitched as he pulled a set of keys from his pocket and unlocked the cuff around the arm of the seat.

A nurse bustled in just then and inserted a syringe into Dakota's IV line, squirting some sort of drug inside. "There, you should be feeling like a new woman in just a few minutes. That will help you sleep tonight."

Dakota nodded to the nurse and when she left turned her attention to Riley. "I won't be pressing charges."

Justus and Kylen shared a knowing look that said they'd seen that coming. But Riley couldn't deny that it came as a relief to actually hear her say it. Hopefully Remington would learn his lesson the easy way this time.

But her hope was short lived when Rem actually had the audacity to pump one fist and exclaim "yes!" under his breath. Riley's hand shot out of its own volition, and this time the slap he took to the head was no gentle tap.

"Ow!"

She cocked one eyebrow. "You deserve that and more. And don't think you have gotten away with anything here. Dad will for sure be hearing about this from me as soon as he gets home."

Justus unlocked the other ring and pocketed the bracelets and Riley practically dragged her brother from the room as he grumbled and rubbed his head.

As she passed Jalen he grinned broadly, then gave her a nod and a wink and a thumbs-up.

She tightened her hand around Rem's arm and

lowered her gaze to the floor, determined not to give the man the satisfaction of knowing she appreciated his support. Thankfully the wedding was over and he and Justus should be heading back to their own side of the state soon. She swallowed, refusing to even give a glimmer of acknowledgement to the whisper of melancholy that thought brought.

And even angrier with herself for giving the man a second consideration.

She turned her thoughts back to her brother. She'd been hoping Remington would learn this lesson the easy way when she knew beyond a shadow of a doubt that not one person in their family was prone to being schooled the easy way. No sir. The Rosses took their lessons the long hard way thank you very much. And woe to any person who latched themselves to a Ross bandwagon along the way, because they were sure to be taken down in the guaranteed fray.

As everyone started to leave the room, Dakota felt a wave of thankfulness combined with a wave of longing to talk to Justus. She knew she'd hurt him the night before, even though he'd been nothing but a gentleman to her this morning. Still, it hurt her a little that he was just leaving without even taking time to say goodbye.

But then he stopped in the doorway, waved to the others, and turned to face her.

Pain radiated through her and she squirmed to

find a more comfortable resting place, determined that it not prevent her from having this talk with him. Besides, she was almost feeling like a new person after whatever drug the nurse had put into her IV bag a moment ago.

He scrubbed the backs of his fingers over his jaw and watched her intently like he had something on his mind but wasn't sure how to tell her.

She had some things on her mind too. She'd only heard part of his story. But she'd heard enough to make her see him differently. He had a good heart. She knew she didn't have to worry about that anymore. If she were honest, she'd known it all along. Even when he'd been running and rebellious he'd had a good heart. She was ready to hear his story now. Ready, so ready, to get to know him better. She lifted one hand toward him.

Someone in the hallway must have said something to him because he turned that way again and spoke. Probably to Kylen, but the combined sounds of the machines surrounding her bed kept her from hearing what he said.

And then he was walking toward her and standing by her side. She reached out and took his hand. "Yes."

He frowned. "Yes, what?"

"I'm sorry I didn't ask to hear your story last night. Yes, I'll have dinner with you."

An emotion she couldn't quite pinpoint entered his expression. "Dakota..."

She smiled. She'd made him speechless.

Heaviness weighted her eyes. "Can we discuss the details another time though?" Her words might have slurred slightly there at the end.

She settled more heavily into the pillow and gave in to the pull of darkness. *Just for a minute.*

A gentle touch against her cheek awakened her. When she opened her eyes the room was dim and no light shone through the window. Puzzlement pinched her brow.

Justus smiled softly. "Sorry to wake you. But I didn't want to leave without saying goodbye and visiting hours are over." He winked. "This nurse is a battle ax and I couldn't charm her into letting me stay like I did the last one."

"I'm sorry. I didn't mean to fall asleep."

"I'm glad you did. Doctor Dallas came through again a couple hours ago. He said your blood work was positive for malaria and they started you on some meds in your IV. Are you feeling better?"

She wrinkled her nose. "Probably by tomorrow. Can I go home?"

He shook his head. "Your fever was over 104 when you got here. They want to keep an eye on you for another day or so."

She suppressed a groan of frustration. "I guess this is not my week."

Justus tilted his head and humor crinkled the corners of his eyes. "It has kind of been rough, hasn't it?"

"I was doing pretty good till you came to town. Hadn't been in the hospital once all year. Never had a tree fall on my house at all before then." She couldn't resist teasing him even though she felt a bit like she'd been on the losing end of a boxing match.

He chuckled. "Har har. Jalen came with me. Maybe this is all his fault."

Dakota tried to smile but only ended up suppressing a yawn. "Yeah. Jalen. Let's blame him." A chill gripped her and she shivered under the blankets.

Justus brushed his fingers over her forehead. "Try to get some rest. I'll see you tomorrow, okay?"

She nodded, her eyes already falling closed. Contentment filled her as she listened to his soft footsteps cross the room.

Riley practically shoved Rem through the front door of her parents' house and then felt a little guilty for the way she was treating him.

Skulking, he stopped and rubbed the spot on his arm where she'd just been gripping him.

Sandy padded in, tongue lolling and tail wagging. Remington dropped to his knees to give her a good scratch behind her ears.

Riley flipped her car keys around one finger and studied the interior of the palatial house she'd been raised in. It sat high up on a large bluff above Marinville and it didn't look any different than the last time she was here. Cold, hard, modern lines spotlessly cleaned by the live-in woman who was housekeeper, cook, and butler of sorts, Lucia. Large windows looked down on the Pacific where the melting sun cast golden molten slag onto the water and horizon beyond. Hanging on the wall opposite the entry was a large canvas of a grotesque, modern art couple, the price of which could probably keep a place like House of Hope running for half a year.

Her lips thinned. Looked like her father's tastes hadn't changed any. Rem shouldn't have to see something like that every day.

She prodded him in the back, nudging him out of the expansive entryway and on into the living room. She bent and patted Sandy on the head as she said, "Hurry up and find Mom. I don't want to leave Jalen sitting out in the car too long."

Her jaw jutted off to one side as she thought of the obstinate man currently waiting in the driveway. Of course she'd had her own car at the hospital, but Jalen had insisted on riding with them here when she'd said she would take Rem home after dropping him off at Serenity Shores.

Stubborn as the year is long. She'd tried to decline. But he'd insisted. And after doing battle with Rem, she hadn't had the emotional energy to fight Jalen too.

She shuddered. This was one place she wished she could have kept her new friends from knowing about. Despite the money sitting in the account Daddy had put in her name, she was by choice practicality penniless and her father was almost a billionaire. It was going to be so hard to explain why she would never ask her father for another dime and why he probably wouldn't give one to her if she did.

Rem headed for the solarium where the wet bar was, and Riley took a breath to ease the rapid beating of her heart. *God, I've tried so hard to escape this place.* She stiffened. Did Dakota and the others even have her talking to God now? He probably wanted nothing to do with her, just like her father.

Remington slumped into the room ahead of her and flopped onto one of the couches, grabbing up the remote on his way down. Mom was lounging on a white leather chaise staring blankly out at the sunset, a martini cupped in one hand.

Rem powered on the TV and a basketball game blared into the room. Sandy jumped up and curled into a comfortable position near his feet.

Mom turned slowly from her perusal and when her gaze settled on Riley her brows rose slightly. She sipped her drink. "Riley. What are you doing here?"

Anyone who didn't know her probably wouldn't realize she was drunk. But Riley could tell by the way she smacked her lips and smiled thinly that she was well on her way to sauced already.

Riley twirled her keys around her finger once and then folded her arms over the pain in her heart. Mom was always perfectly coifed and painted. Her nails were never chipped or in need of color. And she always dressed with a class that emphasized her sleek graceful figure. But beneath all the polish she looked even worse than she had the last time. No amount of foundation could hide the large bags under her bloodshot eyes, the skin starting to sag along her chin, or the wrinkled hands. Alcohol was sucking the life from her.

"I'm here because Rem snatched someone's purse. She is a friend of mine. Luckily she didn't press charges. I'm bringing him home."

Mom fluttered the fingers of one hand. "Lesson learned the easy way then, right Remington dear?" She tittered too loudly.

With her mother's cavalier attitude, it was no wonder Remington thought he could do whatever he wanted. But saying something to her when she was in this state would only do more harm than good. So Riley bottled up the rebuff she wanted to offer and strode over to take in the scenery out the window. The beauty below the house never failed to take her breath away. The modern glass and natural wood home rested above one of the area's few sandy beaches and a path from the backyard meandered down the rocky cliff face, through the beach grass, and onto the expanse of creamy sand before the waves.

How many days had she lain sunbathing on that stretch of beach during summer breaks?

The sun was nearly set now, and where all had appeared set afire from the glow only moments ago, now there were only touches of golden light kissing the rippling crests of the swells. A couple of large rocks just off shore cut black shadows against the water, and the lights of Marinville could be seen off to the left.

She glanced at her watch. She really needed to be going. But she hated to leave Rem with Mom when she was so obviously drunk. "Where's Dad, Mom?" A huff of air escaped Riley's nose. She hated the thought of leaving him with Dad even more.

Mom gave another careless wave of one hand. "Switzerland this time, I believe."

"Actually I'm home."

Riley spun toward the sound of her father's voice, willing away the wash of fear that suddenly had her tasting metal. She wished he didn't still have the ability to make her whole body tremble and her knees go weak.

Sandy leapt off the couch and darted to her bed in the corner, dropping down like she'd been there the whole time. Dad even had the dog cowering in his presence.

Remington jolted upright and powered off the TV, squirming uncomfortably on the couch and pinning Riley with a look that begged for mercy.

She gave him an imperceptible shake of her head to reassure him. She might threaten him with their father, but she'd never actually follow through. Heaven knew Rem had received more than his fair share of "punishment" at the hands of Dylan Ross.

"Oh, you're home dear!" Mom bumbled off the chaise and then tottered on her high heels across the room to Dad's side, but he only brushed her away as he set his briefcase near the grand piano and pulled off his gloves and long winter coat and scarf. Where Mom's glamour looked a little frazzled, Dad was the picture of stoic professionalism. Neatly shaven and pressed, every silvered hair in place. Tie knotted tightly at his throat, even though he'd probably been on an airplane most of the day.

Mom tried not to look hurt by his rebuff and redirected her steps to the wet bar as if that were where she'd been heading all along.

Lucia bustled in to take Dad's things, but he waved her off. "Thank you, Lucia, but I won't be here long. My car is waiting for me outside. I have early business in Portland."

"Very good, Mr. Ross." Lucia disappeared toward the kitchen.

Mom added an olive and a splash of vermouth to her glass. "You weren't supposed to be home till tomorrow, dear. I would have sent Roddy to bring you the Jag if I'd known you would be here today."

"Actually I told you I'd be home yesterday, but the business in Zurich went long and I missed my flight. I just had a car from the office pick me up as I have to be in Portland first thing." Without missing a beat, he spun to face Riley. "Why is there a Mexican sleeping in your heap of a car in our driveway? Please tell me you haven't fallen in with a man of that sort? As if Nate wasn't bad enough?"

Anger shooting through her, Riley studied the

white carpet near her feet. Jalen had been kinder to her in the few days she'd known him than her father ever had been. So if that was the "sort" he was worried about, he could just keep worrying. "Nice to see you again too, *Dylan*." It always grated on him when she called him by his name.

"Don't give me sass, young lady. You may be out on your own, but I'm still your father and you will respect me."

Ruthless. Degrading. It was probably why he had done so well for himself in the business world. But she wouldn't dignify his "discipline" with a reply. She brushed by him. "Actually I'm leaving. I was just giving Rem a ride home from town." At the wet bar, she pulled her mother into a quick hug and then started from the room without a backward glance.

"Riley, wait." Her father's harsh command stopped her in her tracks, but she didn't turn to face him.

"I'm actually glad you are here. There's something I need to say to your mother and it's good you and Remington are present to hear it directly from me."

Glass shattered on the tiles behind the wet bar, and when Riley spun around, her mother's face looked like someone had just painted it white.

Riley felt faint. She knew exactly what her father was about to say and she also knew it was going to kill Mom.

Dad approached it like a business meeting. He

slid his hands into his pockets and turned his back on them to stare into the almost darkness outside. "Katherine, I can't imagine that you haven't seen this coming. I've filed for a divorce. I will be more than generous to you considering you've done absolutely nothing to contribute to our income over the years. Everything should be finalized by the end of the month. You will get this house and a generous alimony. I even imagine you'll still be able to afford the staff."

Despite the fact that she'd seen it coming, shock held Riley in silence.

Mom's voice trembled when she asked, "It's Moira, isn't it?"

Dad's latest hot little secretary, no doubt.

Dad nodded, as if this were a conversation any family could be expected to have on any given day. "Moira and I have purchased a place in Portland. Remington you'll be welcome to come stay with me on the weekends, if you like."

Remington swore one vile curse, and Dad spun around and backhanded him.

"Dad!" Riley lurched forward and inserted herself between the man and her brother.

Dylan Ross leaned over her, eyes bulging. "Don't tempt me to do the same to you!"

"Dylan! Stop!" Mom leaned against the bar like all the life had just been drained out of her. "Just go." The last two words were barely audible.

She wasn't even going to fight it? Of course she wasn't. She always simply accepted what Dad doled out. And it didn't sound like her lifestyle would have to change much, so why would she fight it?

Dad straightened and shoved his hands into his pockets.

Riley's anger boiled into words. She folded her arms. "Don't worry, Mom. You'll probably be better off in the long run."

She saw the moment the anger sparked into action in Dad's eyes.

His face turned a livid red and spittle glistened on his lips. He reached out and grabbed her upper arm, much like she'd manhandled Rem only a few moments ago. Keeping a firm grip, he propelled her across the solarium, through the living room, and out the front door.

Jalen, lounging in the passenger seat, must have heard them coming because he sat up. The lights along the drive illuminated his widening eyes as he took in the man dragging her across the aggregate.

Humiliation burned through her. "Dad stop, please. I'll leave." She tried to extract her arm to no avail.

"You better believe you'll leave! I'm not going to take any more lip from you!"

"Hey!" Jalen was scrambling from her car now.

Terror clawed at her. If Jalen tried to protect her and assaulted her father in his own driveway, he could lose everything. "Jalen stop! Just get back in the car. We're leaving." *Jesus, please don't let my stupidity bring harm to Jalen...*

Dad shoved her hard and she stumbled forward

until she crashed into Jalen's chest. Jalen took her shoulders and set her only far enough away from him to quickly assess her from head to toe. Apparently satisfied that she wasn't terribly hurt, he pulled her close once more in a protective gesture. "It's going to be okay," he said softly, but his gaze drilling into her father's above her head was anything but soft. She'd never seen that look in his eyes before. It was a look that dared the old man to come one step closer.

And for some reason her father stopped. He'd never backed down from anyone before. Dad tossed her keys toward her feet. "Get off my property and take your Mexican trash with you."

Jalen stiffened, but to his credit he didn't respond or retaliate.

Dad spun on one heel and stormed back up the walk.

"You alright?" Jalen's words were low and soft, and his hands slid in a gentle caress from her shoulders to her elbows and back again.

She shivered and nodded, wanting only to get away from this place. She pushed him toward the car. "I'm fine. Let's go."

Her keys had skidded just under the chassis on the passenger side. She dropped to her knees and scrabbled one trembling hand around trying to find them. Finally her fingers settled over the cold metal and she yanked them up. But when she stood and started for the driver's side, Jalen stepped into her path. "Is Remington safe in there?"

She nodded. It was the assurance she always offered. Yes, everything was fine. But in reality she had no idea if Rem was going to be fine. That brought the tears to her eyes.

"Ri." Jalen touched her chin, forcing her to meet his searching gaze. "Do we need to call the police?"

She glanced back to the house. Searched her memory of all the times something like this had happened before. Then returned her focus to his. A tremor washed through her. "I don't know. I think he's about to leave. That's his car." She pointed to the limo idling near the fountain. Its black windows prevented them from being able to see anything inside.

Jalen glanced from the limo to the house and rubbed the back of his head. "Better safe than sorry, don't you think?" He reached for his phone.

Her eyes widened. Was she really about to allow this man to call the police on her father?

"Jalen—"

At that moment the door to the house swung open once more. "You'll hear from my lawyer on Monday!" Dad yelled, and then pulled it shut hard. He stopped when he saw that they were still where he'd left them.

But Riley had already slapped the keys into Jalen's hand and shoved him toward the driver's side of the car. "Let's go. Put your phone away."

Jalen complied, but not before he gave her father one last challenging look above the top of the car.

"Jalen, please."

He sank behind the wheel then and backed them from the drive.

Riley lost her composure halfway down the hill into town. Sobs shook her like an earthquake was rolling through.

Jalen pulled off the road and stopped behind a copse of trees that lined a scenic overlook. He shut off the engine and turned off the cars lights.

A moment later the sweep of the limo's headlights and the gliding black shadow of it against the hillside as it cruised by on the road offered her the sweetest breath of relief. And that only brought on more tears. She jumped from the car and strode over to the split rail fence that set the perimeter of the overlook. Folding her arms against the chill, she closed her eyes and pulled in a long, slow breath, attempting to regain her composure.

The crunch of Jalen's feet were the first thing to alert her that he'd followed.

She dashed at the tears on her cheeks. "I'm sorry. I'm so sorry." A hiccup choked off any more words.

"You have nothing to be sorry for."

She turned to face him. His eyes were dark, soft, concerned. She spun back to study the lights of Marinville far below. "I purposely made him angry. But then when I thought you and he were going to fight, I was so afraid for you that I prayed."

"And God heard you."

Maybe.

The cynic in her was always rising to the fore. But Dad *had* stopped. Of course, who would want to take on Jalen? He wasn't quite six feet tall but he had a good thirty pounds on Nate which put him at about one eighty-five. And it was nothing but muscle. With the way he carried himself all lithe and quiet, Dad had probably been afraid to act further.

"Do you want to go back up to the house now that your father is gone? Make sure everyone is alright?"

No. But she did need to check on Rem. She shook her head. "They'll be fine. I'll text my brother."

She climbed back into the car and Jalen drove them down the hill and turned along the highway toward Serenity Shores.

She pulled out her phone and sent Rem a message. *You both okay?*

Yeah.

What's Mom doing?

Sleeping.

Riley bit her lip and then texted what she knew she needed to say. *I'm sorry I dragged you around by your arm. I shouldn't have done that.* She didn't add that he should not have been such a jerk in the first place.

It's okay.

Call me if you need anything. I mean it. Night.

Night.

She put her phone away and studied the darkness outside her window until Jalen pulled to a stop in front of Serenity Shores.

He put the car into "park", but didn't immediately hand her the keys. He thrust one hand to the back of his neck and hung his head for a moment. She couldn't tell if he was praying or just massaging tense muscles. But after only a moment he looked up and there was such intensity in his expression she held her breath to make sure she didn't miss a word of what he was about to say.

He tilted his head. "Will you do me a favor?"

Without consideration she nodded.

"When you get to your room, read Romans chapter six, starting at verse twenty."

She frowned. "In the Bible?" She felt her face heat and realized how appalled she'd sounded.

Humor softened the intensity of his features, but he didn't laugh or even smile. Instead his gaze swept over her face as though he wanted to remember her like this. "Yes. In the Bible. Want me to show you?"

She shook her head. "No. I'll find it."

Disappointment flashed through his eyes but was gone again so quickly she had to second guess whether she'd actually seen it.

"Okay." He held out her keys to her and when she took them, he captured her hand and gave it a gentle squeeze. "Don't let the devil give you a pay check, Riley."

He left her in the car then, and as she watched

him disappear through the front door she frowned, unable to figure out what he meant.

Once in her room, she waited till she had brushed her teeth and was in her favorite flannel pajamas, then she crawled up onto her bed and pulled out the new Bible she'd been given when she moved into House of Hope last month. She rubbed one hand over the cover. At church she mostly followed along on her phone in an app that Dakota had helped her download. This would be the first time she'd opened this book.

Taking a breath, she cracked the cover. She had no idea where Romans might be but right at the front she found an index that told her what page to turn to. She flipped through until she found chapter six and then trailed her finger down to verse twenty.

When you were slaves to sin, you were free from the control of righteousness. What benefit did you reap at that time from the things you are now ashamed of? Those things result in death! But now that you have been set free from sin and have become slaves of God, the benefit you reap leads to holiness, and the result is eternal life. For the wages of sin is death, but the gift of God is eternal life in Christ Jesus our Lord.

Like a cold bucket of water, the words washed over her. She thought of her family interactions tonight. Of the life she'd lived with Nate. Free from the control of righteousness, for sure. Was she ashamed of them all? Absolutely. Did it feel like they were all enslaved by their poor choices? Totally.

God wasn't responsible, she'd known that all along. It was easier, though, to blame Him for all the pain in her life than to accept that maybe her own sinful decisions, and those of others she cared about, had brought all that pain into her life.

Death... yes, that was exactly what it all felt like.

She reread verse twenty-three.

For the wages of sin is death, but the gift of God is eternal life in Christ Jesus our Lord.

A balance hung before her. Death on one side. Life on the other. She'd been living on the side of death for so long she was a little bit terrified to make the leap over to the other side of the scale.

Don't let the devil give you a paycheck, Riley.

The words suddenly made so much sense.

She bowed her head. "God. I want to be your slave now." She clutched the Bible to her chest and sank against the pillows. She would still have to deal with a lot of the fallout her family would experience because of this night. But somehow she felt a little different. A little more hopeful that they'd all make it through.

Chapter 13

Dakota was released from the hospital Monday morning. She was feeling better, but had no energy to do anything but fall into bed and sleep the whole day through. Riley brought her a bowl of soup for dinner, and after eating it and taking another round of medicine she fell into another exhausted sleep for the rest of the night.

But when she woke up on Tuesday morning she felt like a new person. It was amazing the difference a few hours of the medicine had brought about.

She got up and showered. Dressed in her favorite pair of jeans, a T-shirt, and her faded Seahawks sweatshirt and padded down to the kitchen in her bare feet.

The coffee pot released the heavenly aroma of fresh brew into the air, but no one seemed to be around yet. She poured herself a mug and wandered into the living room.

Darlene sat in a chair near a fire crackling in the fireplace, reading her Bible. She looked up and smiled. "You are looking much better today than you did yesterday when you went up to your room."

"I *feel* so much better. I hope you don't mind that I helped myself to some coffee?" She lifted her mug.

"Of course not. In fact, I was just getting up to make breakfast. Why don't you take this chair near the fire and take it easy until I get it ready?" Darlene stood and tucked her Bible onto the side table next to her chair.

"I could help, if you like?"

Darlene waved her off. "No. No. I'm only making pancakes. That's a one person job, really. And I already laid out the table before I sat down here, so everything is almost all set. I'll call you when it's ready."

Dakota smiled. "Thanks."

She sank into the chair and propped her feet up by the fire. Only a moment later, Alyssa stumbled into the room rubbing her eyes. The moment she noticed Dakota, she scrambled up onto her lap, curling into a ball against her chest.

"Hey there, Munchkin." Dakota rubbed the sleepy girl's back. "How are you this morning?"

"I miss my mommy." She sniffed.

Dakota set her coffee cup down and rocked her. "I'm sorry. She's going to be back in only three more sleeps."

"That's a long time."

It probably did seem like forever to a four-year-old. "Want me to read you a story?"

"Yes!" She was off of Dakota's lap and back in a flash with a colorful picture book full of silly monkeys and laughing hyenas.

She was reading to Alyssa in the funny voice of the jungle python when Justus walked into the room. It must have taken her a moment to notice him, because when she glanced up, he was standing with arms folded and a look of utter amusement on his face. She let the story trail off and grinned, feeling warmth steal into her cheeks.

He tilted his head, and there was something far too intimate in the way he watched her.

"Aunt Kota, the story isn't over yet." Alyssa reached up and patted her cheek to get her attention.

"Breakfast is ready, everyone!" Darlene called from the kitchen. "We'll eat in here at the kitchen table."

"Breakfast!" Alyssa leapt down and made a dash for the kitchen.

Dakota shut the book and set it aside. "Saved by the...griddle, I guess."

Justus chuckled. His gaze swept over her. "You look like you are feeling better. Feel up to a walk on the beach after breakfast?" A hint of seriousness overtook all humor.

"Sure. It will be good to stretch my legs." But even as she said it she couldn't help but wonder if there was more than just a walk on his mind. He must be headed back home soon. They might have missed their opportunity for that date.

Riley and Jalen were already in the Kitchen with Darlene and Alyssa. They were all just sitting down to the table when the doorbell rang. Darlene excused herself to answer it and returned a few minutes later with Pastor Mark. "Look who showed up just in time to get some of my pancakes?" she teased.

Pastor Mark chuckled. "Actually I'm sorry to stop by so early, but I'm here to talk to Dakota and Riley. Could we find someplace to do that?"

Dread settled in Dakota's chest even as she glanced at Riley and nodded. "Sure." This first-thing- in-the-morning call couldn't mean anything good, she was afraid.

She and Riley followed the pastor into the study just down the hall. The man strode to one of the floor-to-ceiling windows and stood quietly for a moment massaging the muscle of one shoulder. Finally, he turned to face them. He looked haggard and tired. There were large dark bags under his eyes and grim lines of weariness etching his lips.

Dakota's heart dropped in her chest. "You don't have good news about House of Hope, do you?"

"I'm afraid I don't."

"Is it as bad as I feared?"

"I'm not sure what you feared, but LoriMay was embezzling money from us."

Dakota clasped interlaced fingers on the top of her head. "Are you sure?" Her voice trembled.

"I'm afraid so. We've had to have her arrested. And she's confessed. She got scared when we brought you on to help her. She was worried she was about to get caught. That's why she quit so suddenly. Unfortunately, it is going to take the church some time to recover from this. We will need to sell House of Hope to try to get the church's funds into the black again."

"What if Dakota and I buy the house?" They were the first words Riley had said all morning.

Dakota's heart went out to her. Of course she was concerned. They needed a place to stay. But… "I don't think that's going to be possible, Riley. I won't have a job now until I can find something." And the only thing she was likely to find in town was not going to shell out enough to pay a mortgage and support both of them.

But Riley didn't seem fazed by her answer. She kept a steady gaze fixed on the pastor. "How much would the church need to sell the house for?"

"Well…uh…" Pastor Mark fumbled through some papers in his briefcase. "The insurance is going to cover all the repairs and of course we'll have to get all that done and inspected before we can sell. But with the amount she has stolen and already spent, we will have to pray God gives us top dollar in order not to be in the red on this. For that reason it's good the house sits right along the beach like it does, it's prime land and pricing for around here." The sum he named made Dakota's head spin.

But Riley didn't even blink. "We'll take it."

Dakota started to protest. "Riley—"

"—I have some cash."

Dakota's eyebrows went up. She'd imagined Riley was penniless when she'd come to live at House of Hope.

Riley pressed her lips together and studied the ground in front of her feet for a moment, then looked up and met both of their gazes. "Can I tell you something?"

Dakota nodded and in her peripheral vision saw Pastor Mark do the same.

"Jalen had me read some verses the other day. They talked about being a slave to sin and how it pays in only death, but that we can choose to be a slave to God and He gives us the gift of life."

Dakota's heart began to beat faster and a spill of joy splashed over the edges of her soul.

Riley's face softened and she folded her arms over her chest in a protective gesture. "I told God I wanted to be His slave."

"Riley!" Pastor Mark strode over and stopped before her, his arms outspread. "That's the best news I've heard all week. Can I give you a hug?"

Dakota was too thrilled to move. She stood stock still and covered her mouth with one hand.

Riley looked uncertainly at the pastor.

He laughed. "It's okay. You don't have to hug me. Just know that you've made one of the best decisions of your life and if you ever have any questions you are more than welcome to come talk to me, alright?"

The redhead smiled tentatively. "Thanks."

Dakota found her feet then and rushed over and

pulled Riley into a hug. She wasn't going to do any asking. "I've been praying for you to do that very thing. I'm so happy for you."

Riley let her cling to her for a moment and then laughed. "There's more to my story."

Dakota released her and stepped back. "Right. Tell us."

"So...um...after I lost..." She laid one hand protectively over her abdomen, but then blinked hard and took a breath as though pushing herself to finish the thought. "The baby. After I lost the baby I was in a bit of a daze, I think. Nate was killed that same night and everything has just been a blur. Both Dakota and Marie were there and urged me to go live at House of Hope. I didn't have the energy to make any other decisions at that point, so I mostly let other people make the decisions that needed to be made. But the thing is...my family is kind of...rich. I had a falling out with my dad several years ago and, well, we haven't been on very good terms. But I have an account with some money in it. I haven't touched it in all these years. But I planned to repay House of Hope once I could get my feet back under me again. And just Sunday while I was at church and thinking about the decision I made Saturday night, I prayed. Well, sort of, it probably wasn't a very good prayer, but—"

Pastor's laugh cut her off. "Any time you are talking to God, Riley, it's a good prayer. Prayer isn't about being all flowery or pious. It's about opening yourself up to your Creator, telling Him your needs and desires, and then allowing him to change you. But go on..."

"Well, I told God that in addition to paying back the church, I wanted to use that money to do something good for Him. This would help the church out, give both Dakota and I a place to live, and maybe we could keep using the house to help other people in need?"

Pastor smiled and Dakota felt another bubble of joy welling up in her.

"It will take time for the repairs to be completed," Pastor cautioned.

Riley only nodded.

"Well then. I don't see why we can't take your down payment to the bank and at least offer it to them. I do have to say they might balk because neither of you are currently employed."

Riley cleared her throat. "Actually. I could pay cash outright." She hesitated. "And still have money to help us rent a place until the repairs are complete."

Dakota felt a little flabbergasted. And Pastor Mark looked like he felt the same.

He rubbed one eyebrow. "Well, I don't want you to rush into this. You could probably find a house in much better shape for maybe just a little more."

Riley nodded. "Dakota and I will talk."

Dakota suddenly didn't care about housing decisions. "Have you told anyone else your good news?"

Riley scrubbed one toe into the carpet and

tightened her lips against a smile. "Not yet."

Dakota grinned. "We should go out and tell them. Everyone is going to be so happy for you."

"Thrilled!" Pastor Mark smiled. "Riley we have a class for new believers at church that I'd like to talk about getting you into, but"—he glanced at his watch— "for now I need to run to an appointment. I'll leave you girls to talk." With that he exited the room and shut the door behind him.

On the heels of such good news, Dakota dreaded what she knew she needed to do next as she stepped across the room. "I need to talk to you about something, actually. I'm sorry I sort of fell apart on you the other night, but I'd like to tell you why."

Riley frowned and folded her arms. "You said you were the girl on the bike?"

"Yes. I was still in high school at the time. My boyfriend's name, as you probably know, was Jason Murton. I was supposed to go back to Africa the next day and just wanted a few more minutes with him. He didn't want to go because we only had the one helmet, but I talked him into it." Dakota massaged her fingers over the tension in her forehead. "So...in a way...it's my fault what happened to Nate. If I hadn't pushed so hard for Jason to take me to Shady Shore..." Tears pricked the backs of her eyes. "Lots might be different today. Your baby—"

Before Dakota knew what was happening, Riley had gripped her gently but firmly by the shoulders.

"Nate's actions are not your fault, Dakota. He was already on the edge. Anything could have pushed him over. And the truth is, much of what he did was probably my fault."

Dakota gripped her friend's forearms. "No, Riley. You can't believe that!"

Riley pulled back with a knowing look and clunked their casts together. "Exactly my point. We're quite the pair I guess, huh?"

Dakota shook her finger at her. "You are slick. Okay, I take your point. But I can't help but feel partially responsible."

Riley nibbled on her thumbnail. "I totally understand that. Maybe we are, in part. I know I feel that way all the time. I lost my baby because I stayed with Nate. Just like you probably wonder what life might be like if you hadn't talked Jason into that drive, I wonder what life would be like if I'd just left Nate like so many people told me I should. If I had, my baby might still be alive. Or if I hadn't moved in with him in the first place I could have saved myself years of anguish." Her voice emerged on a choked whisper. "I wish and wish and wish, but I can't go back and change the decision I made. And I always come back to the realization that Nate has to bear most of the blame."

"I totally know that feeling." Dakota squeezed Riley's arms. "We can only go forward and with God's help, make better decisions next time. But I need you to know that if I could go back and change the decision I made, I would. I hope you can forgive me for the part I played in Nate's degradation."

Riley nodded. "Yes. I can. I do. And you need to know that I might have never listened to Marie and come to church if things with Nate hadn't been so bad. So maybe..." She shrugged.

Dakota pondered that. "We'll never know for sure, I guess. But what I do know is the Bible says God works for the good of those who love Him and are called according to His purpose." Relief spread through Dakota. Now she just had one more person she needed to talk to about that night. "Thank you, Riley. I'm glad we are friends."

Riley seemed choked up by that. "I want you to know that the friendship you and Marie have offered me has made a huge difference in my life. Without that, I don't know if I would have made it."

Dakota pulled Riley into another hug. But no words seemed to be needed.

After a moment Riley stepped back. "So, what do you think about us buying the house?"

Dakota felt her hesitation rise. She didn't want to take advantage of Riley. "I'm honestly happy to help pay a mortgage or rent once I get a job, but I have no savings and no way to help in buying it. I think that will have to be your decision.

Riley turned to look out the window. "Well, buying it would help the church out of a bind. And I like the thought of us being able to help women who need a place to stay."

"Yes, but I don't want you to spend all your

money just so we'll have a place to live."

"I appreciate that." Riley's lips thinned into a smile that said Dakota might not understand everything, but she didn't elaborate further. "I'll think on it and let you know. How's that?"

"Sounds good. Now come on, we have to go tell everyone your good news!" She grabbed Riley's arm and dragged her, laughing, down the short hallway to the dining room, knowing everyone was going to be thrilled with Riley's decision to follow Christ.

Chapter 14

Everyone was as elated for Riley as she'd known they would be and Dakota's heart could not have been more full as she watched Riley grin and try to brush away all their attention.

Jalen tilted back in his chair, his empty plate before him, arms folded over his chest, and a soft smile on his face as he watched Riley speak with Darlene. He was quiet, but Dakota had a feeling based on the amount of emotion reflected in his eyes that he was overjoyed the same as Justus and Darlene, who had already hugged Riley and told her how happy they were.

Dakota layered two pancakes and syrup on her plate, thankful for the return of her appetite.

Justus strode across the room and put his empty plate in the sink. His own mug still in hand, he lifted the coffee pot and one eyebrow, asking her if she wanted a cup.

She nodded and mouthed, "Yes, please" and then let her scrutiny linger as he grabbed a mug from the cupboard, filled it, and added cream and sugar. Today he was wearing a royal blue button-down that brought out the color of his eyes to perfection. He had it tucked into trim black jeans that only emphasized his broad shoulders. She took a slow bite of her pancakes as she studied those shoulders and the lithe ripple of every muscle as he moved. *What would it feel like to have those arms wrap around—*

He turned with a cup in each hand and caught her staring. He stilled. And grinned.

She blushed to the roots of her hair, hoping her thoughts had not been readable, and suddenly took great interest in cutting up the rest of her pancakes.

Only a moment later he set her coffee next to her plate, grabbed a chair and turned it around so he could straddle it backwards, and then set his own cup on the table next to her. He folded his hands over the top slat of the chair. All the while she could feel his watchful study.

He leaned so close that his shoulder pressed against hers, and he spoke low. "I think I liked the look that was on your face just now." The warmth of his breath brushed her ear and heated her face.

She pretended naiveté. "I had a look?"

"Mmmm, you know you did."

She scrambled for an explanation and couldn't help a grin and a coy dip of her lashes. "Must have simply been giddiness at the prospect of having my caffeine addiction fulfilled?" She didn't meet his gaze.

His low chuckle warmed her to her core but she had to know the answer to the question that had been whispering at the back of her mind all morning. "When are you and Jalen heading back home?" She forked in another bite and held her breath.

Justus glance around at the other occupants of the room, then looked back at her and said quietly. "Take that walk with me and we'll talk?"

So he had had another motive when he'd asked her earlier. She nodded and set to work finishing her pancakes.

A few moments later after they'd grabbed their coats, Justus held the door to the back patio open for her and she stepped out into the Pacific breeze. The sun was shining, but the icy wind took her breath away.

"This is too cold for you to be out walking in." Justus looked concerned.

"No, it's fine" She tightened the strings of her hood. "I'm bundled up. And it will really feel good to stretch my legs a bit." She tipped her head for him to follow and headed toward the path that cut along the hillside down to the beach.

They walked beside each other, quietly taking in the beauty of the sun shimmering off the undulating waves below them and the white crests where the surf bubbled onto the shore.

She was suddenly feeling shyer than a ninth grader on her first date. She studied the ground near her feet. He hadn't made any sort of comment to her change of mind about the date. But maybe *he* had changed his. Maybe he hadn't wanted to talk to her in front of the others because he planned to let her down easy. Tell her it had all been a mistake from the get go. And she was too chicken to be the first to speak.

But if he was backing out, what had all that flirting been over breakfast this morning? They left the firm rocky soil of the path and stepped onto the soft sand at the edge of the beach. The tide was out and Justus led her to the firmer ground of the wet-packed sand, but still held his silence.

She chanced a peek at his expression. So serious and thoughtful.

This was silly. She should just take his hand, look into his face, not fall over a piece of driftwood, and ask him what he was thinking. But just as she tucked her lower lip between her teeth and casually reached for his hand, he shoved both his hands into the pockets of his leather jacket. She rolled her eyes and almost giggled. Was this the right thing, anyway? She wasn't really sure.

He stopped and tipped his head to something further down the beach. "Look."

She followed his gaze. Mrs. Murton was walking toward them, a long wool coat cloaking her from neck to mid-calf and a bright red scarf wrapped around her neck and over her grey curls. Her Pomeranian had his ears back and looked like he'd rather be walking anywhere other than the windy Pacific coast.

Mrs. Murton stopped. "Oh, hello. I'm so sorry. I don't mean to intrude on any private time."

"No. No." Dakota hurried to assure her. "We were just stretching our legs."

"Okay." Mrs. Murton didn't look convinced. The elderly lady's gaze flitted to Justus standing by Dakota's side, then she smiled and took in Dakota's lack of crutches. "I'm glad to see you are...moving along a little better."

The woman was referring to a relationship with Justus, and Dakota knew it. She wondered if Justus recognized it too. How many times had Mrs. Murton prodded her to get into another relationship? She chose to pretend ignorance. "Yes. I'm doing great. I haven't needed the crutches since Saturday."

A twinkle lit Mrs. Murton's faded blue eyes. "I meant your relationship with this young man, and you know it."

Justus chuckled and shuffled his feet.

A burn started at the base of Dakota's neck and washed up into her scalp. "We're just friends."

"Mmmm. That's what Jason used to say about you and him." Humor glimmered in her wise old eyes. "I've watched you for years, Dakota. There should be no guilt for you in moving on."

The burn dissipated and left in its place a cold wash of guilt.

Justus settled one hand at her back and leaned close. "I'll wait for you up the beach a ways. Talk to her." With that he turned and strode away.

For a moment as she watched him leave, irritation surged through her. And then she thought of how good it had felt to talk to Riley about it and was reminded she'd been putting this off for far too long. She tucked her hands into the pockets of her coat and doodled her toe across the sand in front of her. She opened her mouth, but shut it again, unsure how to begin. Swallowing, she closed her eyes.

Two hands softly gripped her shoulders.

Dakota dared to look. There was so much understanding and compassion in Mrs. Murton's soft blue eyes that she took a breath.

"I'm sorry you lost Jason so young. But really, moving on is healthy. Good. What God – and Jason – would want you to do."

Dakota shook her head. "Mrs. Murton, there's something—"

"—Gladys, please!" The woman squeezed her shoulders again.

"Gladys..." Dakota licked away the dryness on her lips. There was nothing for it but to just say it. "Jason's death was my fault." Like a tight band had just been unbuckled from around her chest, Dakota felt release.

Mrs. Murton blinked. "No, dear!"

"Yes," Dakota whispered. "I talked him into that ride that day."

Her expression softening, Mrs. Murton tipped her head to one side. "Is that why you've been so tense around me for all these years? We used to have such an easy relationship."

Dakota swallowed and nodded.

The old wrinkled hands slid from her shoulders to her cheeks. "Darling, you were a young girl in love with my grandboy." Her voice choked, but she recovered quickly. "You may have done the asking, and while the choice you both made to get on that bike that day was unwise, I don't blame you any more than I blame him for giving in to you when he knew he shouldn't. Or poor Nate Saunders who was in the wrong place at the wrong time."

"Still..." Tears filled Dakota's eyes. "I'm so sorry."

"Oh, darlin'." Mrs. Murton pulled her head onto her shoulder and stroked her hair. "I've known the whole story for years."

Dakota lifted her head. "You've known?"

Mrs. Murton nodded. "Your mother told us while you were still in the hospital. I should have known that's what's been bothering you. I'm so sorry we didn't talk about this sooner. I forgave you a long time ago, and now you need to forgive yourself."

"I just don't know if I will ever be able to forget. That memory's ingrained so deep it's become a part of me."

"Forgiveness isn't about forgetting, dear. Sometimes one of the hardest things God asks us to do is to live with the consequences of choices and at the same time offer forgiveness – especially to ourselves. But that doesn't mean we forget. It means we choose grace, and mercy, and to offer second chances, because after all, where would any of us be if God didn't give us that first second chance, and that second second chance, and the third, and on and on?"

Dakota nodded and dabbed at the moisture in the corners of her eyes.

Mrs. Murton turned Dakota by her shoulders to face the ocean. "Look at all that water. Could you move it?"

A frown furrowing her brow, Dakota shook her head.

"Of course not. Where would you put it? Now study the waves, and you try and figure out a way to make them stop. What could you do to prevent that next swell from rolling in?"

Dakota pictured herself wading in and trying to keep the waves from hitting the beach. The image almost made her smile. She wasn't quite sure where they were going with this but decided she'd play along. "Nothing."

"Now shut your eyes and listen." Mrs. Murton closed her own and tipped her head back. The wind played with her gray curls on her forehead that had escaped the red scarf.

Dakota watched her for a second more and then closed her own eyes. Far above them one gull called to another. Her feet crunched in the sand as she found her balance. And behind them the beach grass whispered together. But the biggest sound was the *shush*ing of wave after wave crashing onto the shore.

"Oh Dakota dear, there's a song the surf sings. It's constant. Ever moving. Pounding. Relentless."

Eyes still closed, the older woman fumbled for one of Dakota's hands until she pulled it out of her pocket and wrapped the bony, cold fingers in the warmth of her own.

Mrs. Murton continued. "It's a song of grace and mercy, because the ocean is exactly what God's grace and mercy are like for us imperfect people. Always there. Unmovable. Unstoppable. A constant noise begging for our attention, but so repetitive and invariable that it's easy to overlook." Opening her eyes, the woman cast around on the sand before her and then bent and picked up a shiny pink and white pebble. "It's ready to clean and polish and heal. It rubs us up against others to remove some of the roughness of this abrasive world. Takes off all the rough edges and polishes us up."

She returned her attention to the waves and directed Dakota to do the same with one crooked finger. "All we'd have to do is wade in to revel in the power of it. Forgiveness is grace. Forgiveness is mercy. But it's never forgetting. Because it is in the *remembering* that we learn how to make better choices and decisions the next time."

If she had felt like a band had been released from around her chest earlier, now she felt like ten thousand of them had been loosed. She wanted to laugh and cry all at the same time. Grace. Mercy. Forgiveness. The song of the surf. Dakota offered a knowing smile through her tears. "Thank you."

Mrs. Murton squeezed her hand. "Now." She tipped her head toward Justus sitting on a driftwood log down the beach. "You go down there and you tell that young man that if he breaks your heart Spartacus and I will be coming after him."

Dakota laughed. "I'm sure he'll be terrified."

Two grey eyebrows arched. "He ought to be."

"Thank you, Gladys."

Mrs. Murton gave her cheek one more pat. "Go on now." She turned and resumed her trek in the opposite direction from Justus.

Dakota headed over and sank down next to him, tucking her hands into the pockets of her coat to keep them warm.

He cocked one brow. "Feeling better?"

She nodded, even at that moment realizing how much better she really did feel. Her hair blew into her eyes and she reached one hand up to swipe it away. "She said for me to tell you if you broke my heart she and Spartacus would be coming for you."

He laughed outright and shuddered exaggeratedly. "A threat I would never take lightly." His expression turned serious as he studied her.

She bit her lip and reminded herself to breathe.

He broke eye contact and rubbed his palms together. "What did the pastor have to say this morning?"

She sighed and filled him in about LoriMay, and Riley's desire to buy the house from the church.

"She has that kind of money?"

Dakota shrugged. "Apparently."

"I wonder why she didn't just get a place of her own rather than applying to live at House of Hope after..." He let the words that didn't need to be said trail away.

Dakota watched a seagull dart across the sand and considered. "She mentioned that she was in a daze and with Marie and I both urging her to come live at House of Hope, that seemed like the easiest solution at that moment. She needed the companionship and understanding and a place to just land where she didn't have any responsibilities for a while. She's been through a lot and has just been in survival mode. I hardly heard more than two words out of her the whole first week she moved in. I'm so glad God brought her to us."

"It still hasn't been that long. Do you think she's going to be okay?"

"Riley is one of the strongest people I know. Especially now that she's surrendered to God, I think she's going to make it. But I still worry about her."

He leaned his elbows onto his knees and looked over at her. "So what will you do now?"

She hunched her shoulders again. "Not sure. Look for a job, I guess. I've heard the high school is looking for a guidance counselor. And there's always the option to be a grocery bagger down at Thrift and Save." She grinned.

Instead of laughing with her as she'd expected him to, he reached for a stick in the sand by his feet and broke it methodically into small pieces as he studied the horizon before them.

He looked so serious. Like the weight of the world rested on him. She wanted to ease at least one part of that. She pulled one hand from her pocket and rested it on his forearm. Then slid her fingers over the cool black leather sleeve of his jacket until she found the warmth of his palm.

He stilled and returned his attention to her.

"Justus, I'm sorry. I should have just asked for your story the other night. I hope you can forgive me for doubting you. I grew up pretty sheltered. Learning to relate to people who have lived a...rough life can be a little daunting."

He turned his hand palm up, and slid his fingers between her own, then rested his other hand on top, cocooning her fingers in warmth. "How much did you hear the other day in the hospital?"

She tightened her fingers gently around his. "Enough to know that you've always had a good heart."

A muscle bunched in his jaw. "I'm not entirely sure that's true. Only knowing God can make a heart good."

Tilting her head, she said, "Okay then, enough to know that I didn't need to fear going on a date with you. Enough to be thankful that God gives us all second chances." She closed her eyes. "Mrs. Murton was just reminding me about that."

"Dakota..." He dropped his head down and gripped the muscles at the back of his neck. Pain etched his features when he angled a look up at her.

"I'm going to be honest...I'm not sure this"—he swung a finger from himself to her and back again—"can go anywhere. I probably shouldn't have..." He pulled in a breath and studied a cloud floating above them. "The situation with Treyvon took a lot out of me. Sapped my energy for ministry. I was weary and considering quitting my work at Deschutes Rejuvenation and maybe moving here. But..." He shook his head. "God's not going to let me do that yet. Dealing with Remington Ross the other day reminded me of why I do what I do. I have to go back."

Pain lodged like a solid fist just under her ribs. "I see."

She couldn't bring herself to let go of his hand. And he didn't let go either.

"So..." She let her thumb trace over the rough skin of his knuckle. "When do you go home?"

Wind lashed down the beach, sending sand skittering before it. Dakota angled her back and curled her shoulders against the force of it.

"Come here." Justus opened one flap of his jacket and leaned close, wrapping her inside the extra layer of warmth.

Every cell of her body sang with awareness of his nearness as she slid her casted arm behind him; between the warmth of him and the black leather. Her other hand fell to rest just over the rapid beating of his heart. The length of his leg pressed against hers, and his arms clasped together behind her back.

She tilted her head up and looked at him. Blond stubble coated his firm jaw, melding into sideburns that in turn melded into golden wind-whipped curls. A tiny scar angled across his right temple. Blond eyebrows hung low over blue eyes that had almost silver accents.

Those eyes in turn were studying her. His gaze swept over her forehead where her stitches had mostly dissolved away, met her own briefly and then dipped down to pause on her mouth.

She swallowed and licked her lips. He hadn't answered her question. But she suddenly didn't care if he was leaving within the hour – there was no thought for all the complications it would raise if they let this go further...she just wanted him to kiss her, with every fiber of her being.

She curled her fingers into the front of his shirt and tugged gently, tipping her face toward his.

"Dakota," the word was a gravelly whisper as he brought one hand to her face to stop her. His thumb caressed her lower lip and he looked deep into her eyes. "It might be better for both of us if we stop this before it starts."

She kissed his thumb, she couldn't help herself. Her own words emerged low and raspy. "Once I decide I want something, I'm pretty hard to deter. I'm also pretty good at long distance relationships." Her lips trailed to his palm and she dropped another kiss there.

His eyes fell closed and he swallowed visibly. "I might be really bad at them though."

She quirked an eyebrow and teased him with a kiss to his jaw line. "Then it will be a good thing you'll be far away, because I won't be able to kill you." His stubble prickled her lips and tantalized her with the hunger for more.

A chuckle rumbled from his chest and, as she leaned forward to drop another kiss along his jaw, he turned his head and pressed his lips to hers.

Perfect bliss. That was the only way she could think to describe what she was feeling just then.

His lips were smooth and soft. And the kiss was only the softest of caresses before he pulled back. His thumb stroked over her cheek, and his gaze roamed her face. Then his focus dropped to her mouth and a low sound escaped his throat. Swiftly, he captured her lips with his own, fully, firmly, flagrantly.

She could feel the steady beat of his heart beneath her fingers. Hear his rapid breathing. Taste the yearning for this never to end that hung between them.

But it did end. Because all too soon he eased back and pressed his forehead to hers. She gulped for air and he did the same. A tremor shivered through her. "Justus—" She inched away far enough to ensure she could get a good look into his eyes. "Maybe I can try to get a job near you? Near Deschutes Rejuvenation?"

He shook his head. "I thought of that, but Dakota, I don't want you in danger. My job is...tough. Gritty. Draining. And sometimes I work with boys who'd like nothing more than to get at me in some way. I don't want to put you in the middle of danger. And I certainly don't want you near in a case like that."

She pouted softly. "I could be tough if I needed to be..."

He shook his head and gave her a quick peck before pulling back again. "No. I couldn't live with the risk I'd be putting you in."

She wanted to wheedle and plead. She could talk him into it, she felt sure. But she stopped herself. She certainly didn't want to create a situation where Justus might get hurt trying to protect her. And there was still Riley to think of. "Okay, but I'm going to miss you." She rested her forehead against his chin and contemplated just how true those words really were.

Finally, she leaned back and looked up at him. "When do you leave?"

His eyes were soft, contemplative, full of an emotion she couldn't quite pin down. "We're heading out tomorrow morning."

"So soon." Dread seeped through her. She rubbed one finger over the middle button of his shirt. How had he enraptured her so quickly?

He bent down to intersect her line of vision. "How about that dinner I asked you to? You and me? Tonight? Maybe even a little dancing." He pumped his eyebrows twice.

She giggled and angled forward to whisper conspiratorially, "I'm a great dancer. This amazing guy taught me. And he did a pretty good job if I do say so myself." She covered her mouth and the laugh that wanted to burst out. "So long as we don't dance anything but a waltz."

His chuckle was warm and soft. "I bet a smart lady like you would pick up any steps to any dance fairly quickly. Especially if an *amazing* guy was doing the teaching."

"How about right now?" She took his hand and stood, pulling him out to the relatively firm dance floor of wet sand. She stepped into the circle of his arms and wrapped her own around his neck, peering up at him. "We'll dance to the song of the surf."

"The song of the surf?"

"Mmmm. Something Mrs. Murton said." She tipped her head in thought. "The ocean is a reminder to us of the vastness of God's grace. Always washing in, ready to clean us up and give us a fresh new start. Second chances. New beginnings."

His hands settled at the small of her back. "I think I could use a refresher course in that." A soft seriousness glinted in his eyes. "I told you about Treyvon. I need to go visit him. I've been putting it off."

"I know what that's like – putting something off – so I'll just say that you'll feel better once you go."

"I have no doubt you are right." He eased out a breath. "I'll go see him as soon as I can." Soft emotion shone in his eyes as he studied her. "Dakota, I'm not sure where this can go. What the next step is for us."

She batted away his hesitation with a flip of her wrist. "Maybe we don't always have to know what the next step is. Maybe we just give ourselves to the dance and see where it takes us?"

"Doesn't sound like much of a plan."

She nodded. "But maybe it's the only plan we've got."

He lowered his head and kissed her lingeringly. "I'm game if you are."

"I've enjoyed every dance I've ever had with you. I don't see why this one will be any different." She purposely stepped on his toe.

He laughed. "It's an adventure already."

Epilogue

Justus stepped out of his car and eyed the imposing building before him for a long moment, hands resting on his hips.

He'd been home for a week, and had already put this off longer than he should have.

Dakota had been chiding him softly via text messages to do this ever since he'd arrived back home. He grinned and shook his head. Already, he couldn't imagine his life without her in it.

He pulled the visiting order out of his back pocket and smoothed it open. He handed it and his I.D. to the guard on duty. The man checked him off and waved him through to wait in the visiting area.

Treyvon blinked when they brought him in and it was obvious the guard hadn't told him who his visitor was. "Mr. Teague." He stopped, seemingly unsure whether he should sit down or not. "I'd 'bout give up. I didn't never expect to see you again."

Sorrow washed through Justus. "I'm sorry about

that, Trey. I really am. I needed some time, but I should have been here much sooner than this. How've you been?"

The boy sank into the seat across from him and started talking, and Justus knew he was exactly where he was meant to be.

The visit was too short. They always were. But he did his best to offer Trey words of encouragement, forgiveness, and hope before the guard came and indicated it was time to head back to his cell. Trey's eyes held a question. "You gonna come again, Mr. Teague?"

Justus nodded. "I'm going to be here every chance I get from now on, Trey."

"Thank you." Moisture glistened in the boy's eyes, but he blinked hard and spun on his heel, dogging the guard's footsteps out of the room.

Back out in the parking lot, Justus sank into his car and pulled out his phone. *I did it. It was hard. But really good at the same time.*

Yay! So proud of you, Dakota responded, followed by a pair of smoochy lips.

He grinned. *I'm going to hold you to that kiss the next time I see you.*

She sent a succession of the smoochy lips and then ended with, *ha ha.*

Now you are just torturing me.

The next emoticon was an animated one that pumped its eyebrows. *Just doing what I do best.*

He sighed and dropped his head back against the seat rest. This long distance thing was going to be torture. And the term had just started. He didn't see himself having time to get away again until Thanksgiving. But he was glad they were giving it a shot. He didn't know how God was going to work this relationship out. He only knew their future was in His hands. And for now, that was enough.

For now.

Excerpt from *Written in the Sand,*

Pacific Shores, Book 4
Coming Summer 2015

Chapter 1

Riley Ross set her bags of groceries from the Thrift and Save into the back seat of her old Jeep and glanced at the time on her phone. She yanked open the driver's door.

Of course Mom couldn't have given her any more than five minutes' notice that she needed Rem picked up from soccer practice today, because that would be too much to ask.

From the slight slur in Mom's voice when she'd called, Riley would be willing to bet her last dollar Mom was keeping a barstool warm, and a healthy tab running, down at Pete's. And why was it Mom hadn't arranged to have Rem picked up in the first place? Mom couldn't even drive right now. But had she thought ahead to ask Roddy, their groundskeeper, to plan to get him? No.

Riley just hoped Mom had been telling the truth about taking a cab. *The last thing I need to deal with is Mom getting pulled over for driving under the influence.* Especially since her license was currently revoked from the last incident.

A huge sigh slipped free. This was the first day of soccer for Rem. And she supposed it was going to become her regular responsibility to pick him up each day. Because it was seemingly beyond Mom's capability to get her son to and from the places he needed to be when she was so busy helping gravity with its job of keeping the chaise lounge firmly on the floor at the house. Or instructing Lucia, the live-in maid, what meals to prepare and what rooms to clean. Or apparently equally taxing, keeping Pete in business.

Riley grimaced at herself in the rearview mirror as she pulled out onto the two-lane coastal highway in front of the grocery store and headed toward the high school. "Stop it." She gave herself a pointed look.

It was too easy to let her frustrations with her mother's behavior make her forget that it was all a mask to bury the pain Mom refused to face. Heaven knew Riley had tried to get her to counseling on more than one occasion. And had talked to her about moving on until she was blue in the face.

Jesus, it's going to take something big to reach her, I'm afraid.

Thankfully, Riley's job as a second-grade teacher's aide had regular hours. She got off at four o'clock each day. So it wouldn't be too much of a hardship to swing by the high school and pick up Rem and run him up to the Bluffs. She reminded herself how thankful she'd been when she heard he'd decided to play soccer. She hoped it would keep him from finding too much trouble this year. The way Rem was always trying to prove himself to everyone had her just a little bit terrified of what he might get involved in during this his first year in high school. She'd heard the school had hired a new coach. Hopefully, he would be a guy who had his head on straight and not one of those macho jerks who would teach his kids to obliterate the opponents no matter what.

The late August sun beat down unmercifully and Riley could feel sweat dampening the armpits of her light blue silk top. She lowered all four windows and let the breeze cool the interior of the car. At least her hair was up in a bun off her neck today, not that the wind was probably doing her any favors in that department. But the only thing on her schedule for tonight, after dropping Rem at home, was to change into jeans and head over to finish up some of the remodeling to the house on Second Street, so it wasn't like it mattered what she looked like.

She whipped into the high school parking lot and stopped in a slot close to the soccer field. She could see the team doing cool down stretches near the far goal, but couldn't pick out who Rem's coach might be from this distance.

She propped her elbow against the window and rested her head against her fist. Her eyes slid closed. Five a.m. had been a long time ago. And she still had a lot of work left in her day. Maybe she could catch a few minutes of rest while she waited.

Birds twittered lustily from the shade of the maple off to her left, and somewhere high overhead she heard the shrill cry of a gull. The sun beat down on her head warming her and only increasing her drowsiness. An insect droned by and the wind slipped through grasses and leaves, whispering tranquility and peace. All the details blurred into a soft haze.

Riley's head fell off her fist and jolted her awake. She blinked and focused. The team was standing now and several players were already near her in the parking lot loading their sports bags into vehicles and laughing and joking with one another.

She scanned the field for Remington, but didn't see him anywhere. He might be expecting Mom to pick him up from the parking lot on the other side of the pitch. Riley sighed and rolled up her windows, then climbed from the Jeep and slung her purse over one shoulder as she clicked the locks into place. She should have thought to ask Mom if they'd predetermined a place to meet. Not that Mom would have necessarily remembered if they had.

She rubbed the back of her neck, willing away the last vestiges of sleepiness as she picked her way up the low grassy hill to the level of the field.

She sheltered her eyes with one hand as she scanned the players, searching for Rem's red mop of curls. Finally, she spotted him, still in the center of the field twirling a soccer ball around with his feet while he apparently engaged in a conversation with...

Riley froze where she stood. She felt the heels of her pumps sink into the soft moist soil at the edge of the field, but couldn't seem to move. Her hands fluttered to her hair and she could feel even without the aid of a mirror that the disarray would be hopeless to repair.

She sighed. Her mouth was dry. And all thoughts of sleepiness fled. In fact, her heart was beating so hard anyone might have thought she'd just been running a 5K instead of napping in her Jeep.

And all because of the sight of the man talking to Rem. The man with the whistle hanging around his neck. The man who was quite obviously the new soccer coach at Marinville High.

Jalen Rivera.

She shook the surprise away and focused on the simple happiness washing through her, instead. Jalen was the reason she'd finally seen the Truth that God loved her and wanted her to serve Him. The reason she was serving Him today. And without Jesus to lean on over the past few years, she didn't know where she would be right now. She thought back to what her life had been like not long before she met Jalen for the first time, and shuddered. Thankfully, God had helped her put those memories behind her little by little over the last couple years. And that had all started because of Jalen – well, Marie and Dakota and Taysia had a big part in her salvation story too.

She couldn't be happier that Rem was going to have such a great coach. She just totally hadn't expected to see him here. Or her reaction to seeing him here.

Slowly, she eased her heels from the dirt and started toward them.

Her thoughts turned to the past and the promise she'd made herself. The night Nate had beaten her so badly she'd lost their baby, he'd left the house in a drunken rage and wrapped himself around a rock along the Pacific Highway and killed himself. After that night, she'd promised herself she would never be so vulnerable to the power of loving a man again.

And then she'd met Jalen. He'd only been in town for a short time for Reece and Marie Cahill's wedding, but Riley had felt more of a connection with him in that short time she'd known him than she ever had with any man previously. But he'd had to go back to his job on the other side of the state.

Jalen had texted with her for a few months after he'd returned home, but then, to sever ties with some of her old friends who were not such great influences, Riley had changed carriers and her number. She'd thought about reinitiating contact numerous times, but her newfound commitment to remain single had always kept her from doing so.

Now she took a breath. It was great to see him again, but she needed to keep up her guard.

Because if ever there was a man who could tempt her to give up her vow, it was Jalen Rivera.

And...her hand skimmed over her abdomen... For his sake it was best she remember that and keep her distance.

Jalen bent and grabbed up his towel from the bag near his feet and scrubbed at the sweat coating his forehead and hair as he smiled at Remington Ross. The kid had shot up quite a few inches since the last time Jalen had seen him two years ago, when he'd been in town for Reece Cahill's wedding. He was still scrawny as all get out, and short for his age, but that didn't bother Jalen in the least. The kid could control the ball like few his age, and from what he'd seen today, Rem had a good understanding of the positions of the game. And it was obvious his interest went beyond just an understanding to an actual love for the sport, as evidenced by the fact that while most of the team had already meandered off the field, Remington was still here pacing through some footwork.

Jalen slung his towel over his shoulder and rested one hand on the kid's shoulder. "Nice job out here today. You have a real knack for the game."

What he really wanted to talk about was Remington's older sister. The woman who was the reason he'd come back to Marinville in the first place. Was she faring better now that some time had passed after the death of her abusive boyfriend? Was she seeing anyone? Jalen scooped up his sports bag. Please, heaven forbid, she wasn't married was she? But he held all those questions inside. Time would reveal the answers. Time would tell him whether he was simply a fool lingering over memories of a woman who had somehow captured his heart in a few short days, or whether something could actually come of it.

Remington bent and picked up his ball, resting it against one hip as he eyed Jalen. The expression in his eyes said he wasn't quite sure whether to take Jalen's compliments seriously.

Jalen nodded. "I mean it. I was impressed with what I saw today. But I hope you won't let that go to your head because the whole team has some improving to do."

Remington shrugged. "Sure. I get ya."

"Good. So I'll catch you tomorrow, okay?" He waved goodbye and turned to head for his car in the parking lot. He stilled, his heart rate kicking up as though he hadn't just spent the last fifteen minutes cooling down.

Picking her way toward them from the edge of the field, one small hand shading her eyes, was Riley. Black slacks. A silvery blue blouse. Red hair piled into a messy knot at the back of her head. And – he swallowed – looking even more beautiful than he remembered.

Take a breath, Rivera. He did that, and then forced one foot in front of the other in what he hoped looked to be a casual stroll across the field and not something similar to the dashing, dancing, and leaping of joy his heart was doing in his chest.

He stopped a few feet before her when he

suddenly realized he probably smelled like a field horse after a long day of plowing. He resisted a grimace. Good thing the breeze was brisk so the odors wouldn't linger around. "Riley." He offered her a smile.

"J-Jalen." Her face looked stricken, but she followed up quickly with "It's so good to see you again!" She stepped toward him, intent on pulling him into a welcoming embrace.

He jumped back. "It's good to see you too, but I probably smell like the wrong end of a mule right about now." He nearly clenched his eyes shut. *Talk about smooth, Rivera. Way to leave her with such a charming picture.*

"Of course." She offered the reassurance, but her tone said she thought she'd somehow offended him. "I'm sorry, I didn't mean to—" Her gaze searched out his left hand where it still gripped the towel slung over his shoulder and she stuttered to a stop and let the rest of the sentence trail away, then dropped her gaze to the grass at their feet.

His own gaze searched out her left hand where she twirled her car keys nervously. No ring, at least.

A herd of wild mustangs on the run must have taken up residence in his chest. When she'd cut off contact with him, he'd been discouraged. But he'd decided to honor her obvious wishes. But something about this woman wouldn't release his thoughts and he didn't think a day had gone by that he hadn't wondered how she was doing. He'd weaseled information out of Dakota a few times, but it had never been enough. So, for two years he'd been waiting and praying. Wanting to come back and pursue Riley, but never feeling it was quite the right time.

And then he'd seen the ad for the high school soccer coach—or rather Dakota had sent it to him in an email with a little winking face and no other comments. The email had arrived the day after he and Justus had learned that the funding for their ministry, Deschutes Rejuvenation, had dried up and the church that had been sponsoring the program was cutting it. He had a feeling that cutback had answered a few of Justus's prayers as well as his own. They both had been willing to continue serving, but both of them had been serving with divided hearts for the past couple years.

The breeze tugged at the golden-red strands of Riley's hair and he noticed that the sun had brought out a few light freckles across the bridge of her nose. Seeing her again made him feel like an out-of-oxygen scuba diver breaking through the surface of the water and pulling in that first life-giving breath of air.

"So you're here to pick up Rem—"

"—So you're the new soccer coach."

They spoke at the same time, and then smiled at each other sheepishly.

She tilted her head. "I hadn't heard you were back in town?"

There was something different, *less vulnerable,* about her countenance. "I just got here last night.

They interviewed me on Skype since the last term at Deschutes Rejuvenation was still going."

"Dakota told me your funding was cut. I'm sorry about that."

He shrugged. His years in that ministry had been good. Blessed. But there wasn't a place he would rather be right now than where he was standing. "Was time to move on, I guess."

She spun her keys around one finger. "Where are you staying?"

"Reece has given Justus and me a room at a discount out at Serenity Shores Bed and Breakfast, for now. But we're looking for a place to rent."

"I see. Well, I can tell you I'm very pleased that you'll be Rem's soccer coach."

She tilted her head and smiled fondly at him, but it was a smile that suddenly had him second-guessing his plan to make his feelings known to her, because the gesture was sisterly. Cordial. Platonic. Guarded.

She tucked a wisp of hair behind her ear. "I'd better get going. It's nice to see you again, Jalen." She looked past him. "Rem, Mom asked me to pick you up. Let's go, please."

"Just a sec!" Remington called back, continuing to dribble the ball toward the soccer goal at the far end of the field.

Riley opened her mouth to call him again, but her phone rang and she paused to dig it out of her purse. She glanced at the caller ID, a small frown forming on her brow.

He should go and leave her to her call in private, but after seeing her for the first time in two years, he wasn't quite ready to deprive himself again so soon. Especially since this might be the most interaction he'd ever get with her.

She pressed on her screen. "Hi, Kylen, what's up?" The furrows on her brow deepened as she listened. "I'm at the school picking up Rem from soccer practice, why?" Her hand went to her forehead. "She what?" Her eyes fell closed. "Was anyone hurt?" A breath left her in a long, slow exhale. "Well, thank God for that. I'll get Rem and...we'll be down in a few minutes, I guess." She blinked hard. Then blinked again. "No, don't be sorry. This is not your fault. We'll be there as soon as we can." She hung up and stood staring at her phone for a long moment, as though she wished she could go back a few minutes in time and not answer it.

He shouldn't intrude, but he went against his better judgment and asked, "Everything alright?"

She looked up as though coming back from someplace far away. "Uh...no, but thanks for asking." She stretched her lips, but it didn't come across like much of a smile.

He reached out and squeezed her shoulder before he thought better of it. Then snatched his hand away. He tipped his head toward the boy still practicing shots into the net. "I'll get him for you." Turning, he jogged toward Remington, wondering what news Kylen, one of Marinville's four police officers, would have been calling her about. Jalen knew her father had left the family to move in with his secretary in another city a couple years ago, and her mother hadn't been doing well even before that. *Lord, whatever it is, give her the strength to make it through. Let me help her through it, if I can.*